OUT OF

THE BLACK

OUT OF
THE BLACK

JOHN RECTOR

Text copyright © 2013 John Rector
All rights reserved.
Printed in the United States of America.
No part of this book may be reproduced, or stored in a retrieval system, or transmitted in any form or by any means, electronic, mechanical, photo-copying, recording, or otherwise, without express written permission of the publisher.

Published by Thomas & Mercer
PO Box 400818
Las Vegas, NV 89140

ISBN-13: 9781477805046
ISBN-10: 1477805044
Library of Congress Control Number: 2012923929

For Amy

In the dream, I do everything right.

I hold her hand a little tighter. I press my lips against hers a few seconds longer. I ask her not to leave, not quite yet.

And in that brief pause, everything changes.

She still smiles at me, like before, and she still kneels down to zip Anna's jacket and make sure her hat with the pink tassels is covering her ears. She still touches her cheek to mine and whispers, "Good luck," before she takes Anna's small hand in hers and walks out into the cold.

I still watch from the doorway as she helps Anna into her seat then walks around and climbs in behind the wheel.

And when she drives away, she still waves good-bye.

Except this time, it's not really good-bye.

This time, things are different.

This time, she doesn't make the light on Twelfth Street. Instead, she sits at the red and listens to the radio and watches in the mirror and smiles as Anna dances in her seat and tries to sing along.

And this time, when the light changes from red to green, she pulls out into an empty intersection. There are no screeching brakes, no shattering glass, no twisting metal. There are no faraway screams of sirens, and there are no flashing lights, and there is no phone call.

In the dream, she comes home.

In the dream, I get to hold her again.

In the dream, I do everything right.

PART I

1

Once Jay was done talking, I lifted my drink and finished it, then motioned to the bartender for another.

"So, what do you think?" he asked.

"I think you're out of your fucking mind."

Jay's smile didn't fade, but the light behind it dimmed fast. He turned back to the bar and the television mounted above the pool table in the corner. "That's what Roach told me you'd say."

"She was right."

"It's a good plan, Matt. I've been over all the angles. It's going to work."

"You're serious about this?"

"Hell yeah," he said. "An opportunity this good? It'd be a mistake to say no."

"Then I guess I'm making a mistake."

Jay stared at me. "So that's it? You'd turn your back on me just like that?"

Before I could answer, the bartender came by with my drink. I paid him from a shrinking stack of bills in front of me, and he counted them on his way back to the register. I watched him ring up the sale, but when he slid the money into the cash drawer, I had to look away.

Easy come.

Jay was staring at the TV. His lips were moving, and I knew he was still arguing with me in his head. I'd been friends with him long enough to know he wasn't going to let this go until he felt he'd had his say, maybe not even then. I decided to get it over with.

"Why come to me?"

Jay ignored the question and pointed to the TV. "You really don't see it?"

"See what?"

"He's soft, Matt. Just watch him."

I looked up at the screen. The local news was on, no sound. The man they were interviewing was old and carried a polished black cane. His hair was short and silver, and the lines on his face cut deep.

The reporter walking beside him looked young enough to be his granddaughter. She listened as he spoke, sometimes nodding, always smiling, and held his arm in hers as they crossed through a slow, shaded green garden somewhere in the city where things still grew.

I didn't recognize the spot.

"He's old," I said. "That doesn't mean soft."

"He's trusting."

"How do you know that?"

"Because even with all that money, he still lives in a small house right outside of town, no security." Jay shook his head. "I bet he keeps his money in coffee cans."

"I'm guessing he doesn't."

"Either way, he's an easy target. He's not going to risk his wife by going to the cops, not over what we're asking."

"What are we asking?"

"Five hundred."

"Thousand?"

Jay nodded. "Split down the middle."

I laughed.

"Laugh all you want, but that kind of money doesn't mean anything to him."

"You really believe that?"

"Of course I do."

I shook my head. "What does Roach think?"

"It was her idea."

I looked down and stirred my drink with a thin red straw. "Why doesn't that surprise me?"

"His wife comes into the salon every two weeks, always alone. Roach works the front counter and makes all the appointments. She can get us times, dates, all of it."

I'd already heard the pitch, and I didn't want to sit through it again, but if I didn't stop him, he'd keep going until I'd had enough and walked out. That was just the way Jay was. He never could take no for an answer.

"You know what it sounds like to me?" I asked.

"What's that?"

"It sounds like you want to go back to prison."

"Over this?" Jay smiled, leaned in close. "No, this is easy money. The plan is rock solid. We can't lose."

"Anyone can lose."

"Not this time."

I spun the ice around the bottom of my glass, then took a drink and motioned to the TV. "What did he do?"

"No idea," Jay said. "A new wing down at the gardens? Or maybe a school for homeless orphans?" He shrugged. "It doesn't matter. The local news eats all that charity shit up."

"I meant his money. How did he make it?"

3

Jay looked at me, and at first I didn't think he understood the question. Then he said, "Is that important?"

I thought about it. "I guess not."

Jay took a pack of cigarettes from his pocket and tapped one out. "From what I heard, he inherited it."

"From who?"

"His father?" He put the cigarette to his lips. "His grandfather? Some dead relative made a fortune drilling oil in South America. I don't know the specifics."

"Oil drilling?"

Jay lit the cigarette with a black Zippo. "Could be bullshit, but it's what I've heard."

I leaned against the bar and studied the old man on the screen. He didn't look rich. In fact, nothing about him screamed money. His clothes were plain, wrinkled from the day, and his sleeves were pushed up past his wrists showing faded green tattoos underneath.

"You sure this is the right guy?"

"Doesn't look like much, does he?"

"No," I said. "He doesn't."

"That's because he doesn't give a shit about his money, and that's why this'll work." Jay tapped his cigarette over the red plastic ashtray. "I mean, what's the point in having that kind of cash if you're not going to spend it?"

I told him I didn't know.

"If it was me, you'd never see my face around here again."

"I don't know," I said. "Home is home."

"When did you get so Goddamned sentimental?" Jay laughed then put the cigarette to his lips and inhaled deep. "What would your old Semper Fi buddies say?"

I smiled, silent.

The interview with the old man ended and was replaced with a familiar shot of police cars, flashing lights, and yellow crime-scene tape surrounding a low house on the south side. The tagline along the bottom of the screen was only two words.

Bodies found.

I watched for a while then turned away and ordered another drink. When the bartender set it in front of me, I reached for my money, but Jay put his hand on my shoulder, stopping me.

"I'll get this one." He pulled a credit card from his pocket and handed it to the bartender. "Run a tab?"

The bartender took the card and walked away.

Jay yelled after him. "And we'll take two more."

"Who the hell gave you a credit card?"

"I applied for it," he said. "They give them to anyone these days."

"Obviously."

Jay finished his drink in two swallows and set the empty glass on the bar. When he did, I saw his hands were shaking, but I pretended not to notice.

"I want to ask you something," I said. "And I want you to tell me the truth."

"You got it."

"Why me?"

"We have a history."

"Car stereos and shoplifting," I said. "And not since we were kids. You've never come to me with something this big."

"I thought you could use the money. And since we go back, I figured—"

"Don't give me that shit."

"What do you want me to say? You did this kind of thing when you were a soldier. You know what you're doing."

"Marine."

"What?"

5

"I wasn't a soldier," I said. "I was a Marine."

"Is there a difference?"

I took a drink. "A pretty fucking big one."

Jay hesitated. He crushed his cigarette in the ashtray and said, "Whatever, Matt. The truth is you're my friend, and you have a van."

I laughed. "There it is."

"We'll switch the plates. Don't worry."

I didn't know where to begin, so I kept quiet.

"Look, I know you'll have my back, and I know you'll do what you say." He tapped out another cigarette and lit it. "I trust you."

"Is that it? Trust?"

"What else is there?"

It was a good answer, but not good enough.

"Sorry," I said. "Count me out."

Jay waved me off. "You're not going to say no."

"I think I just did."

"You'll change your mind."

"And why's that?"

"Because you're my friend, and I need your help."

"You think that's enough?"

"It would've been at one time."

I stirred my drink, watching the kaleidoscope of light from the back bar reflect off the slow-melting ice. "You know I can't do something like this. It's not who I am."

Jay turned to face me. "I need this, Matt. We both need this, and you know it."

There was an edge to his voice that bothered me, and it made me want to argue, but I couldn't.

He was right.

"I made promises," I said. "I can't break them."

"Promises? To who?"

6

I didn't say anything. I didn't need to.

Jay looked down at the wedding ring on my finger and frowned. "You're still wearing the ring?"

I nodded.

He sighed, deep, shook his head. "All right, I'll lay off, for now. This isn't what tonight was supposed to be about anyway." He took a drink. "Five years inside. We have a lot to catch up on."

"It's been a long time."

Jay turned and lifted his glass. He held it up between us. When I didn't reach for mine, he frowned.

"Come on, for old times?"

I picked up my glass. "What are we drinking to?"

Jay seemed to think about it for a moment, then he smiled. "To ghosts."

I didn't like the toast, but before I could say anything, Jay reached out and touched his glass to mine. The sound, delicate and sharp, hung in the air around us like a curse. I didn't want to drink to it, but in the end, I did anyway.

"Okay," I said. "To ghosts."

2

Jay kept buying the drinks, and the next few hours spun together in a blur of smoke and laughter. I was over my limit and thinking about calling a cab when Jay said, "Another round?"

I told him I'd had enough.

"One more," he said. "It's not like you have to be at work in the morning."

He laughed, but I didn't.

"Jesus, it was a joke." He leaned across the bar and waved to the bartender, holding up two fingers. "You used to have a sense of humor."

"When was that?"

Jay reached for his cigarettes and tapped one out. "Fifth grade? Hard to remember now."

I watched him put the cigarette to his lips. His hands were trembling, and he fumbled with his lighter. I took it and lit it myself.

Jay leaned into the flame. "Thanks."

"You doing okay?"

"I'm fine."

I started to ask more, but then the bartender came over and Jay ordered two more drinks and a couple shots of Jameson. I tried to stop him, but I didn't try that hard.

When the bartender left, I turned to Jay and watched him sway on the stool. His hands moved constantly.

Eventually, he noticed.

"What?"

"You're using again."

"The hell I am."

I frowned. "Who do you think you're talking to?"

"I swear it." He put the cigarette in his mouth and held it there, then stood and pushed his sleeves up past his elbows. "Nothing, not since before I went inside."

His arms were scarred, but that was nothing new.

It meant nothing.

I'd seen him like this before, and I knew all the signs. Even though the veins on his arms were clean, I was willing to bet the ones on his legs told a different story.

I looked away. "It's your business."

"What do you see?"

"Nothing."

"That's right." Jay sat back down, silent.

A minute later, the bartender brought our drinks. I reached for mine, but Jay didn't move. He was staring up at the TV, his jaw muscles working under his skin, and he didn't seem to notice.

"Come on," I said. "Last one?"

Jay didn't look at me.

"You can't blame me for having doubts," I said. "Not after all we've been through."

"It's not that."

"I don't believe you."

"There it is, right there." Jay shook his head. "I *always* believe you, no matter what. If you tell me something, I trust you." He paused. "And if you ask me for a favor, I do it."

"What's your point?"

"My point is that I'd go out of my way for you, but when I need your help, you brush me off without a thought."

"Is this about the old man again?" I shook my head. "You didn't really think I'd say yes to that, did you?"

"I thought you might, but that's not what bothers me."

"Then what?"

"You and me, we have a huge opportunity here, life changing." He motioned to the TV. "It's right there for the taking, and you're going to miss it."

I looked up at the screen. The old man was on again, cane in hand, walking through the same shaded garden with the same blonde reporter.

"Oh, shit."

"What?"

"They're replaying the news." I picked up the shot of Jameson and slammed it. "I've got to get home. I'm late."

"You're leaving?"

"I have to."

"But it's still early. We have drinks."

I told him I was sorry, then took my coat from the barstool and slid it over my shoulders.

Jay watched me for a moment, then got up and grabbed his jacket. "We'll share a cab," he said. "My treat."

"I'm on the south side."

"Doesn't matter."

I pointed to the TV. "No more talk about this shit."

He held up three fingers, swore.

"Why don't I believe you?"

Jay smiled and grabbed his cigarettes from the bar. He motioned to the door and said, "Shall we?"

I nodded and followed him out into the cold.

• • •

The street out front was wet and lined with snow-dusted cars. I pulled my coat tight around my chest while Jay stood on the corner and tried to hail a cab.

One stopped, and we climbed in the back. I gave the driver my address and started to close the door when I remembered the tab.

"Shit, your card."

"My what?"

"Your credit card. You left it inside. You didn't sign for the tab."

Jay looked back at the bar and waved it off. "I'll come by tomorrow and sign it. They won't care. I know the owner."

There was a familiar catch in his voice, and I frowned. "Are you kidding me?"

"What?"

"That wasn't your card."

Jay smiled, pointed to the open door. "Close that so we can go. It's freezing."

I slid out of the cab.

"Where are you going?"

"To pay the tab."

"I thought you said you had to get home."

"I'm not skipping out on it."

Jay said something to the driver then angled over in the seat to face me. "I told you, I'll come back tomorrow. I do this all the time."

I stayed on the sidewalk by the cab and let the snow fall heavy around me. I looked down at my watch and tried to make a decision, but all I could think about was Anna waiting for me at home.

Jay was lying. I knew he was lying, but I also knew I didn't have the money to cover our tab and the cab home.

The driver said something to Jay, who held up his hand and said, "Make a choice, Matt."

I took one last look back at the bar and told myself I'd come by tomorrow to settle the tab. Part of me knew it wasn't true, but it was enough to get me moving.

I stepped off the curb and climbed into the cab.

Once I closed the door, the driver pulled out. I watched the crowds pass outside my window, thinning as we approached the highway. Then they were gone and there was only snow.

I glanced over at Jay. He was leaning back on the seat with his eyes closed. At first I thought he'd passed out, but then he opened his eyes and stared at me.

"What?"

"I'm going to say one more thing," he said. "Then I'll let it go."

I leaned back. "My answer isn't going to change."

"I want you to think about it, that's all."

"Jay—"

"Just consider it." His voice was flat, cold. "Weigh your options before you decide. We've got time. Look at it with an open mind. If your answer is still no, I'll let it go and never bring it up again, I swear to God."

"You don't have to wait for my answer."

"Am I really asking too much?"

I started to tell him that it was pointless, that no matter what, my answer would still be the same.

But before I got the chance, Jay leaned in and whispered, "We're talking about a quarter of a million dollars, Matt." He smiled. "Each."

I don't know what it was, but something about those words caught me off guard, and for a moment I let myself imagine what I'd do with that kind of money. I thought about how much different life would be, and once all the possibilities started flashing through my mind, it was tough to push them away.

I turned and stared out the window at the city lights passing cold and bright behind a swirling wall of snow.

"I'll think about it," I said. "But that's all."

"That's all I ask."

"Don't expect me to change my mind."

"You got it," Jay said. "No expectations."

We didn't say anything else the rest of the way.

My mouth tasted sour, and I could smell the smoke from the bar on my skin. It was all making my stomach turn, so I leaned back and closed my eyes and listened to the buzz of the tires passing over the road.

I thought about Anna, and home.

3

The cab pulled up in front of my house. I took the last of my cash and handed it to the driver. Then I turned to Jay and said, "Good to have you back."

Jay looked past me at the house. "This is your place?"

"That's right."

He stared for a moment longer. "Are you sure you don't need the money?"

"'Night, Jay."

"You'll think about what we discussed, right?"

"Sure," I said. "I'll think about it."

I got out and shut the door and watched the cab pull away. I waited until it disappeared around the corner, then I opened the gate and walked up the cracked cement path to my front door.

The house was dark except for a soft glow coming from the kitchen window. I knew that Anna would be asleep by now, and that Carrie would be inside, waiting.

Knowing this made me feel even worse.

I slid my key into the lock and went inside, moving as slow and silent as possible. I took off my coat and set the keys on the table by the door and headed toward the light in the kitchen. Halfway there, I saw a shadow shift on the couch, and I heard a voice.

"Matt?"

"It's me," I said.

Carrie sat up, her eyes half-closed. She tucked her hair behind her ears and stretched. "What time is it?"

"Late."

"Is everything okay?"

"Everything's fine," I said. "Lost track of time."

"I figured." She looked around. There was a library book lying open on the end table next to a half-empty cup of coffee. She picked up the book, marked her place, and closed it on her lap. "Did you have a good time?"

I had to think about my answer.

"Yeah," I said. "I guess I did."

"You must've. What did you two talk about?"

"He offered me a job."

Carrie's eyes went wide. "That's great."

"Not that kind of job," I said.

It took her a moment, but then the understanding spread over her face. "Oh." She paused. "But he just got out of jail. Why would he—"

"I don't think he was serious," I said. "He talks big, but nothing ever comes of it."

"I guess that's good."

"He's part of a different life, that's all."

"There's only one life," Carrie said. "Just different chapters." She got up and stepped closer, then reached out and touched my arm, soft. "I'm happy you're home safe."

I looked down at her hand. Her skin felt good against mine—too good—and for an instant, all I wanted to do was reach out and pull her close and kiss her.

But I didn't.

Instead, I moved away.

Carrie smiled, but it never touched her eyes.

We stood, neither of us saying a word, then Carrie motioned toward the window and her house across the street. "I should go. I'm sure you're tired."

I nodded. "Thank you again."

"It was fun," she said. "Oh, and someone called for you. He didn't leave a number, said you'd know what it was about." She picked up her coffee cup and started toward the kitchen. "I wrote it down. Brian something."

I felt a cold burn start deep in the center of my chest. It hung there for a moment, then sank.

I tried to ignore it.

Carrie came out of the kitchen with a yellow sticky note and handed it to me. "He said he wants to see you, but he didn't leave an address."

I read the note then crumpled it. "Thanks."

"Who's Brian?"

"A friend of mine," I said. "He owns Murphy's, down on Sixth Street."

"Brian Murphy?" Carrie folded her arms across her chest. "It's not Brian Murphy, is it?"

I didn't answer. "It's late."

"Matt?"

"What do you want me to say?" I thought of Anna asleep in her room and lowered my voice. "He's an old friend, and he helped me out a while ago."

"Helped you out?"

I paused. "I would've lost the house, Carrie."

"You borrowed money from Brian Murphy?"

"It wasn't my first choice."

"I hope not." She put a hand to her chest. "What about me? I would've lent you the money."

"You don't have the money to lend."

"I could've found it," she said. "And you wouldn't end up dead in an alley if you couldn't pay me back."

"I'm not going to end up dead in an alley," I said. "I'll pay him back."

"It's not him I'm worried about," she said. "Do you have any idea who he works for?"

"I know," I said. "And I'll handle it."

Carrie started to say something else, but instead she put a hand to her mouth and turned away.

"Go ahead, say it. You might as well."

She shook her head. "No."

"You don't think I'll be able to pay him back."

"Let me lend you the money," she said. "You can settle with him and pay me when—"

"No."

"—ever you can."

"I don't want to do that."

"What you don't want is to owe these people money."

"I don't want to owe money to anyone," I said. "That includes you."

Carrie stopped talking and turned away. "I should go. I'll stop by in the morning and walk Anna to school."

"I'll take her," I said. "Don't worry about it."

"Are you sure?"

I told her I was.

Carrie nodded and grabbed her coat from the arm of the couch. I stood by the door, watching her slide it on, and tried to think of something else to say, but all I could do was stand there and hold the door as she walked out.

When she got to the bottom of the steps, she stopped and turned back. "Just so you know, I gave her a camera. It's an old Polaroid I found. She really loves it."

"I bet she does."

Carrie started to turn away.

This time I stopped her.

"How was she tonight?"

"She missed you."

I nodded, ignoring the empty feeling the words left behind, and said, "Other than that."

Carrie took a deep breath and let it out slow. "We worked on her reading and her numbers and she did great. She's progressing, Matt. I think she's going to be fine."

I smiled and felt my throat get tight. For a second I couldn't speak at all. When I finally found my voice, all I could say was, "Thank you."

We stood for a moment longer, silent, letting the snow fall soft and slow around us. Then Carrie raised one hand and turned away, crossing the street to her house.

I watched her until she was safely inside. Then I stepped back and closed the door.

• • •

Anna's room was at the end of the hall. I stopped outside her door. There was a new handwritten sign tacked halfway up that read *No Boys Allowed!!!* Then underneath it, in smaller letters, the words *This means you, Daddy!*

I smiled and pushed the door open.

The light from the hallway slid across the room. Dash, Anna's Jack Russell, was lying at the foot of the bed. I could see the two white spots on his back, and I thought about the day I brought him home, and how Anna had said they looked like big snowflakes—the same but different.

She was right.

I stepped closer, and Dash growled.

I put a finger to my lips and shushed him.

He growled louder, showed teeth.

Anna was on her side, asleep, with one arm slung over her head. I sat on the edge of the bed next to Dash, who made one last growling effort to scare me off. When it didn't work, he got up and moved to the other side, away from me.

I lifted Anna's arm away from her face and watched her sleep. The light from the hallway shone warm against her skin. I reached up and ran my finger along the scar just above her eyebrow, tracing the jagged pink line until it curved and disappeared under her hairline.

Anna stirred. "Daddy?"

Dash sat up, grunted.

"I'm here, baby." I brushed the hair from her face. "Go back to sleep."

"I waited for you."

"I know." I leaned in and kissed her forehead, soft. "I'm home now."

She rolled over, and her eyes drifted shut.

I stayed with her until I was sure she was asleep. Then I got up and walked out, closing the door behind me.

4

I turn off the shower and I can hear her in the room. I pull back the curtain. She's standing at the sink, leaning into the mirror, tracing the thin lines around the edges of her eyes with her fingertip.

I say, "You're beautiful."

She says, "I swear these weren't here yesterday."

I reach for my towel and wrap it around my waist. The air is warm and wet and I can smell the morning coffee drifting in from the kitchen where Anna is eating her breakfast and singing.

Beth is wearing her blue dress, the one I love. The fabric is thin, faded by wear, but the way it slides over her skin when she moves makes me ache inside.

I stand behind her and run my hands down her back, stopping at her hips. Then I press against her and kiss her neck.

She makes a warm sound, closes her eyes.

"Do you have to go?" I ask.

"Yes."

I breathe against her neck, my lips barely touching her skin. "I wish you didn't."

"I'm sorry."

I kiss her again then reach down and slowly lift her dress up over her hips.

"Hey."

A whisper.

Beth pushes back, and the sound she makes burns through me in the most perfect way.

"I love you," I say.

Beth breathes hard, leans forward. As she does, a drop, like a single tear, falls dark and lands red in the clean white sink.

Then another.

I stop moving and watch her in the mirror. Her head is down, and her hair falls forward, covering her face.

She doesn't speak.

"Are you okay?" I ask.

More drops, and now the sink is red with blood.

I step back and move the hair from her face, still watching her in the mirror. "Hey, look at me."

Beth lifts her head, slow, and at first, all I see is the blood. Then I notice her eyes, dark and rimmed with shadows, staring out at me from behind a veil of hair.

I step back, feeling the scream build inside me.

Beth smiles, showing rows of dark, broken teeth.

Again, I want to scream, but the only sound I hear is the cold rush of air in her throat as she opens her mouth and—

"Daddy?"

• • •

"Daddy?"

I opened my eyes.

There was a click, a flash, and I was blind.

I sat up fast, kicking the sheets away. "What the—"

Anna laughed, and the tiny motor in the camera spun. "Look what Carrie gave me." She set the camera on the bed and pulled the swirled gray photo out and handed it to me. "This one's for you. It takes a few minutes."

"Thank you." I felt a sharp pain behind my eyes, and my heart was pounding heavy against my ribs. "Are you hungry?"

"I made toast." She looked at me, frowned. "You stayed out late."

"Yes I did."

"Are you hungover?"

It wasn't a question I was expecting, and definitely not one I was ready to answer, so I didn't. "What did you and Carrie do last night?"

Before she could say anything, the phone rang in the kitchen. Anna picked up her camera and looked down at Dash waiting by her feet. "Come on, boy."

She ran out, and he followed, his nails clicking across the floor after her.

Once she was gone, I leaned forward, elbows on knees, and rested my head in my hands. The pain was fading some, but the dream was still fresh in my mind. I closed my eyes against the images and tried to will them away.

I knew that eventually they would fade—they always did—but never fast enough.

I heard Anna pick up the phone, but I didn't move until she called me. "Daddy, it's Grandpa."

"Shit."

I eased out of bed and looked around for my pants. I found them on the floor in the corner of the room and slid them on. Then I grabbed a clean shirt from the drawer and walked out into the kitchen and the start of my day.

Anna was standing at the counter with a box of dog treats in one hand and the phone in the other. Dash was at her feet, jumping up and down, whining, but she was focused on the phone and didn't seem to notice.

"No, he's here," she said. "I love you, too. Okay, bye, Grandpa." She handed me the phone.

I covered the receiver with my palm and said, "Go get ready for school. We'll leave in a minute."

"Okay." She held out a treat for Dash, who devoured it in two bites. Then they both disappeared down the hallway.

I closed my eyes and put the phone to my ear. "Morning, Jerry."

"She sounds good today. Got a spark in her voice."

"She's getting there," I said. "Better every day."

"That's wonderful, Matt." He paused. "How about you?"

"Good days and bad."

"You don't sound so good."

"Long night." I grabbed a glass from the cabinet and filled it with water. "Listen, I've got to walk Anna to school. Was there something you needed, or can we—"

"Just checking in," he said. "I wanted to see how the job hunt was coming along. Any luck?"

"Not yet."

"Sorry to hear it."

There was no trace of sincerity in his voice, and I could feel myself start to say something I knew I'd regret. I managed to stop before I did, but the urge was still there. I put the glass to my lips and drank until it was empty. Then I filled it again.

"Any prospects?"

"No," I said. "I'll hit the labor office after I drop Anna at school. Maybe I'll get lucky. If not, I'll keep looking."

Jerry exhaled, long and slow. "Have you given any more thought to what we discussed?"

A thin stab of pain formed in the center of my head, and I closed my eyes. "No, and I'm not going to."

"It wouldn't be permanent," he said. "Just until you're back on your feet."

"No, Jerry."

"I'm only thinking about what's best for Anna. It's not—"

"I know what's best for Anna."

"Of course you do, but let's be honest about the situation. You almost lost your house. You two were one step away from living out of your van."

"It never came to that."

Jerry hesitated. "Not this time."

"It never will. I took care of it."

"I never said you don't do what needs to be done. You're a good father, Matt, but everyone has rough patches. All we want to do is help."

I felt the anger build inside me, and I pushed it back the best I could. "Thanks, but we're fine."

Jerry was quiet for a moment. When he spoke again, his voice was soft. "I'm afraid Dorothy is going to insist."

I laughed. "Let her. It doesn't change anything."

"Matt, I—"

"Anna is my daughter. She stays with me."

"Dorothy's not going to let this go."

"She'd better."

"Matt." He paused. "You and I both know we have a strong case. The lawyers we've talked to—"

"The lawyers?" I started to say more, but Anna was in the next room, and I didn't trust myself not to yell. "You have lawyers now?"

"Anna's well-being is important to us, and we'll go as far as we need to go. Don't make us drag everything out into the light over this. That won't be good for anyone."

"Jesus, Jerry."

"Once you're back on your feet—"

"I haven't been on my feet since the accident. There are no jobs out there. What makes you think that'll change anytime soon?"

"Because it has to," he said. "Even if it doesn't, I know what kind of man you are. You'll figure it out."

"What kind of man is that?"

"The kind that will do whatever it takes to keep his family together."

"You mean what's left of it."

The second the words were out of my mouth, I regretted them. Jerry didn't say anything, but I could tell I'd hit a nerve. Part of me felt bad, but it was a small part.

"Tell me something, Jerry," I said. "If Beth were still alive, would you two still be doing this?"

"I don't understand."

"I'm asking if you and Dorothy are pushing so hard to take my daughter because you want to fill the hole left behind after yours died."

"This has nothing to do with Beth."

"Is that true? Because it looks—"

"Goddamn it, Matt." Jerry's voice shook. "We're trying to do what's best for our granddaughter, that's all."

"You keep saying that."

Jerry was quiet. "It doesn't have to be this way. We're on the same side. Let us help you."

"I'm fine," I said. "We're fine."

"I don't think I believe you."

"I don't care what you believe," I said. "I won't let you take my daughter."

Jerry took a deep breath. "Matt," he said. "I honestly hope we don't have to."

5

Anna held my hand all the way to school, and she didn't say anything until we stopped out front and I knelt down to give her a hug.

"Why were you fighting with Grandpa?"

"We weren't fighting," I said. "We were having a discussion."

"About me?"

"About a lot of things."

She looked down, silent. "I don't want them to take me away from you."

"What?" I reached out and lifted her chin. There were tears in her eyes. "Nobody is going to take you away."

"I heard you tell Grandpa—"

"They want you to come stay with them for a while, that's all."

"What about you?"

I tried to smile, but it didn't work. "No, not me."

"What about Dash?"

"I don't think Dash would let you go anywhere without him, do you?"

Anna seemed to think about it for a moment. Then she said, "He'd like it up there. Lots of squirrels to chase."

"How about you?" I asked. "Would you like it there?"

She shook her head, slow.

"Are you sure?"

"I want to stay with you."

"Then you'll stay with me," I said. "Just the two of us."

"And Dash."

"Right, the three of us."

The bell rang. Anna stepped closer and wrapped her arms around my neck. "I've got to go now. Bye, Daddy."

"Bye, sweetheart."

She kissed my cheek and ran up the steps to the front of the school. When she got to the doors, she looked back and waved.

Then she was gone.

I stood outside for a while longer as crowds of parents and kids shuffled past me. Then I looked at my watch and started walking.

The labor office handed out the day's jobs first thing in the morning, and once they were gone, they were gone. If I wanted to work, I had to hurry.

The nearest bus stop was two blocks over. I was halfway there when I saw Jimmy Murphy standing on the curb, leaning against a familiar black-and-gold Chevy Tahoe.

For a second, I considered turning around and finding another way, but it was too late. He saw me, and as I got closer, he stepped out and opened his arms, as if welcoming me home.

"Matt Caine." He smiled, showed teeth. "Just the man I'm looking for."

"I don't have time, Jimmy."

"No problem," he said. "I'll walk with you."

I knew I didn't have a choice, so I kept quiet.

"You know, Brian thought coming down here would be a waste of time, but I had a hunch you'd be around sooner or later." He motioned back toward the school. "You can avoid phone calls, but you can't avoid school days, am I right?"

"What do you want?"

"Just checking in." He took a wrinkled brown cigarette from behind his ear and lit it as we walked. "How's life treating you these days? Last time we talked, things weren't so good."

"Better now."

"Good to hear it," he said. "You paid those bills you were worried about? Kept the house?"

I told him I did.

Jimmy nodded. "I've always thought it was important for all of us to stick together. You know we were worried about you."

"Thanks."

"Hard times for everyone these days," he said. "It must be even tougher with a kid to worry about."

I stopped walking, stared at him.

He raised his hands. "We're just talking."

"Then make your point."

Jimmy put the cigarette to his lips and inhaled deep. "Shit, this isn't going the way I hoped. I'd like to start over. Can we do that?"

I waited.

"I came down here to pass along a friendly reminder to pay back the loan. You're coming up on two months, and—"

"I know how long it's been."

"—things are starting to pile up."

I looked at my watch, started walking again.

Jimmy kept pace. "I thought you should know that Brian is concerned. And since you're not returning his calls—"

"Tell him it's coming."

"He'll be happy to hear it," Jimmy said. "I'll let him know you'll stop by this week. Sound good to you?"

"It won't be this week."

Jimmy hesitated. "I feel like I should remind you that the vig doubles next week. After that, we start getting into some serious—"

"Fuck, Jimmy." I turned on him fast but he didn't flinch. "I know what I owe, and I told you it was coming. That's what you need to tell your brother. If he has a problem with that answer then he can get off his ass and come talk to me himself next time."

I turned away, but Jimmy grabbed my arm.

His grip was strong.

I looked down at his hand then up at him.

Jimmy let go, and when he spoke next, his voice was even and calm. "I'm glad you're aware of the situation, Matt. That makes this a lot easier. Some people I have to explain things to."

"Not me."

"No, not you," he said. "But I don't think you're seeing the entire picture."

I started to say something, but Jimmy held up his hand, stopping me.

"When you don't return Brian's calls, or when you yell at me out here like this for everyone to see, word gets around." He pointed to the row of walk-ups lining the street. "Most people around here don't know our history. They don't know that Brian will tolerate shit from you that he won't tolerate from them."

"Not my problem."

Jimmy nodded. "You're right, it's not your problem. It's mine, and it's Brian's." He held up one finger. "But if you don't settle this account soon, it'll be a problem for all of us. Do you understand what I'm saying? Because I need you to tell me you understand."

"Yeah," I said. "I understand."

Jimmy took another drag off the cigarette then flicked it end over end into the street. "Brian can only do so much. Eventually, the partners are going to start asking questions, and then all of this will be out of his hands." He paused. "When that happens, I'd hate to be the one to have to come find you."

There was a tone to Jimmy's voice I'd never heard before. It wasn't threatening, and it wasn't angry, it was something worse, something almost desperate. If I hadn't known better, I might've thought he was begging. Whatever it was, the words sat cold inside me.

"Are we done?" I asked.

Jimmy stared at me, his face even, emotionless. "You never change, Matt, do you?" He leaned in close. "Call him and talk to him. Work something out. He'll listen."

I didn't say anything.

"He can't keep covering for you. If word gets around that you're taking advantage, he won't be able to help you."

"Yeah? And where would that leave us?"

Jimmy's eyes narrowed, and his smile seemed to slide across his lips. "Is that a serious question?"

I stared at him and tried not to blink.

"Tell him it's coming," I said.

Jimmy nodded. "I hope so, my friend. I really do."

6

I made it to the labor office right as the doors were opening. I got in line and was given a spot on a cleanup crew at a new construction site just outside the city. There were eleven of us, and we spent the day clearing a scatter of cement blocks, gathering broken boards, and tearing down two hundred feet of rusted chain-link fencing. By the time we finished, every muscle in my body ached, and my hands were blistered and bloody.

I made sixty dollars.

We climbed back into the truck, and they dropped us at the labor office just as the sun was slipping below the horizon. I walked home, feeling each step, and thinking about Anna.

Carrie would've picked her up from school that afternoon, and by now they'd have finished her lessons and were probably waiting for me. I thought there was a chance I'd make it home in time for dinner, but even if I didn't, I'd still get to see Anna before she went to bed.

There was never enough time.

After the accident, I wouldn't leave Anna's side. She had no memory of what'd happened, and that was a blessing, but some nights it would come to her in dreams and she'd wake up screaming, calling for Beth.

Those were the nights I'd crawl out of bed and stumble down the hall to her room. I'd hold her in my arms and rock her back and forth, and I'd tell her not to be scared, that I was there, that I'd always be there.

It was my promise to her.

If she needed me, all she had to do was call my name and I'd come running, forever and always, no matter what.

Eventually Anna would stop crying and she'd fall asleep. I'd tuck her back into bed then take a blanket and pillow into her room and sleep on the floor by her feet.

I told myself I was doing it for her, that if she woke up again, I didn't want her to be alone. But there was more to it. With Beth gone, my bed was just too big.

• • •

By the time I got back to my neighborhood, the sun was down, and the snow had started again. I could see my house at the end of the block, the light from the windows glowing gold among the shadows and snowfall.

I put my head down and kept moving.

When I got to the house, I unlocked the door and stepped inside. The air was warm and sweet.

"Something smells good."

Dash barked, and Anna ran out of the kitchen. She was wearing a lime-green apron and holding a wooden spoon covered in thick chocolate. "You have to see this," she said. "We made cupcakes."

I took off my coat and walked into the kitchen. Carrie was standing at the counter spreading frosting over the tops of the cupcakes, her hair pulled back in a loose bun just above her shoulders.

When she saw me, she smiled.

"We wanted to surprise you."

"It worked," I said. "I'm surprised."

"They're chocolate," Anna said. "Your favorite."

I put my hand on her head. "I can't wait to try one."

"They're not ready yet." Carrie turned to Anna. "How about showing him your pictures?"

Anna's eyes got big. "Do you want to see them? I took a lot today."

"I'd love to."

Anna smiled and dropped the spoon in the sink. She ran out to the living room, and Dash followed.

I opened the cabinet above the sink and took out a mason jar and unscrewed the lid. There were several bills inside, and I added the sixty dollars I'd made.

"How was your day?" Carrie asked.

I told her it was fine, then said, "Thank you for your help. You didn't have to do all this."

"Are you kidding? I never get to bake." She nodded toward the doorway. "And she had a great time."

"It's more than tonight," I said. "I don't know what I would've done this past year without you."

"She's a sweet girl, Matt. It's no trouble."

"You've helped her so much," I said. "She loves you."

Carrie set the frosting knife down and wiped her hands on a frayed dish towel. She looked up at me, her eyes green and clear. She started to say something, then stopped and leaned in fast, pressing her lips against mine.

I didn't pull away. Instead, I reached up and touched her cheek, felt her skin, breathed her in. It felt so good that I didn't want to stop.

But I did.

"Carrie, I—"

Carrie bit her lower lip and turned back to the counter and the tray of cupcakes. I saw her chest rise and fall with her breath.

I reached out and put my hand on her shoulder. "I'm sorry, I—"

She shrugged me off. "Don't worry about it."

A minute later, Anna came back carrying a red shoebox filled with Polaroid photos. She set the box on the kitchen table and started taking the photos out, one by one.

"You've been busy," I said.

I flipped through the photos as she handed them to me. Most were of Dash in her room, some were of Carrie sitting on the couch with a book open on her lap, and the rest were random shots from outside.

"I think you have a photographer on your hands," Carrie said. "She's unstoppable."

I smiled and kept sorting through the photos. One caught my eye and I slid it out of the pile and held it up to the light. It was of one of the feral cats from around the neighborhood. This one was orange and black, and it was crouched next to the fence by the alley. Its head was turned toward the camera, eyes reflecting red, and it had something heavy and gray in its mouth.

I held it out to Anna. "What's this one?"

She looked at it. "That's a cat."

"I got that," I said. "What's in its mouth?"

"A rat."

I looked closer. At first I didn't see it, but then I noticed the claws and the thin black-wire tail.

Something rotten settled inside me.

"This was out back?"

Anna nodded, never looking up from the photos. "Over by the fence."

"There are rats out there?"

"I started seeing them over the summer," Carrie said. "I'm surprised you haven't noticed them."

I flipped through a few more shots of abandoned homes, barred windows, and overgrown lawns, each photo looming larger than the last. It occurred to me that I was seeing Anna's world, the world I provided for her, through her eyes.

The realization weighed heavy in my chest.

I looked through them all before going back to the one with the rat. There was so much I wanted to say, but I didn't know where to begin.

Anna must've noticed, because she smiled, said, "It's okay, Daddy. They leave you alone if you leave them alone."

I cleared my throat and tried to keep my voice calm. "You just stay away from them, got it?"

Anna nodded.

I dropped the photo on top of the stack and leaned back. For a while, nobody said anything.

Carrie held up one of the cupcakes. "Who's ready?"

I didn't feel like eating anything, but then Anna looked up at me, her eyes wide. "You want one, right?"

"Of course I do."

Carrie handed me one of the cupcakes, and I stared at it for a moment before stuffing half of it in my mouth.

Anna's eyes went wide. "What do you think?"

I smiled, showing chocolate-covered teeth. "It's delicious."

Anna laughed.

The sound was so happy and so genuine, that for one fading moment, despite it all, the world was perfect.

7

On the day the letter arrived, Anna was outside with Dash. She was building a snowman with what little snow was left on the ground while Dash ran in circles around her, jumping, barking.

I stood at the window with the letter in one hand and the phone in the other, trying to calm down. I had to call Jerry, but I was forcing myself to wait. At that moment, all I wanted to do was put my fist through a wall. I knew if I didn't take some time, I'd only make things worse.

I watched Anna for a while longer, then turned away from the window and sat at the kitchen table. I unfolded the letter in front of me. It was from a law firm upstate telling me they were starting custody proceedings. They were asking me to consider Anna's best interests and willfully sign over guardianship to her grandparents.

I read the letter twice, then dialed Jerry's number.

He answered on the second ring.

I asked him about the letter, and somehow managed to keep my voice calm. I don't know how, but I did.

"It's all in there," Jerry said. "I don't have anything else to add."

I picked up the letter and read it out loud. When I finished, I said, "Her best interest? When have I ever done anything that wasn't in her best interest?"

"That's not—"

"Answer the question." My voice was loud, but I couldn't help it. "When have I ever done anything where she wasn't right up front in my mind?"

"I told you," Jerry said. "We're only trying to help."

"By taking my daughter?"

"No one is taking anyone."

"Then what the fuck do you call it?"

Jerry pulled the phone away, covered the receiver, and said something off the line. When he came back, his voice shook. "I'm going to put Dorothy on."

"Goddamn it, Jerry, don't—"

But it was too late. Before I could get it out, Dorothy was on the line, her voice bright, cheery, and completely insincere. "Hello, Matt."

"I want to talk to Jerry about this."

"I'm afraid you have me instead," she said. "Jerry isn't feeling well today, and this is a stressful situation for everyone involved."

"Am I supposed to feel sorry for him?"

"A little understanding would be nice," she said. "Perhaps if you took a step back and looked at our side of things, you might see why we're doing this. Maybe you'd even see it our way."

"Your way?"

"One second, Matt." Dorothy lowered the receiver. I heard movement and a door closing. Then she was back. "I'm sorry, but I don't want Jerry hearing any of this. He really is in knots over the entire thing."

"He should be," I said. "And so should you. What you're doing is unforgivable. At least Jerry knows it."

"We're doing what we think is best for Anna, and make no mistake about it, Jerry feels the same way I do. It might be hard to face, but for the time being, she will be better off here with us."

"Bullshit."

"Is it, Matt? Is it bullshit?"

"This family has been torn apart enough."

"Yes, it has, but that doesn't change the situation you're in right now."

"My situation is temporary," I said. "Money is tight, but that's no reason to—"

"This isn't just about the money."

"Of course it is," I said. "It's the only thing you have to hold over my head. It's your only weapon."

"Matt—"

"If it's not the money, then what is it?"

Dorothy paused. "Are you still having the nightmares?"

I opened my mouth, but all that came out was a short, choked sound. I felt a rush of anger sweep through me, and I closed my eyes and waited for it to pass.

It took a while.

"Yes, I know about the nightmares," Dorothy said. "And the mood swings, the violent behavior, all of it."

"It's not like that anymore." My voice sounded unsure, even to me, but I kept going. "You don't know what you're talking about."

"I know Beth was scared of you. I know she would call me in tears almost every night those first few months after you came home. She told me what you—" Dorothy stopped. "She told me what happened over there, so I know more than you think."

I thought back to that time, and as much as I hated to admit it, Dorothy was right. I'd put Beth through more than I ever wanted to in those days, and I wasn't surprised to hear she'd turned to her mother when things got really bad.

Still, it hurt to hear.

"It's different now," I said. "Those dreams have stopped. Things are better."

"I'm glad," Dorothy said. "But that's only part of the larger issue. What about Anna? She's still recovering from the accident. She needs special attention."

"I know what she needs."

"But does she get it? From what I hear, she spends most of her time at home with one of your lady-friend neighbors."

"Her name is Carrie," I said. "She's a nurse, and Anna loves her."

"That's all well and good, Matt, but Anna needs tutors and counseling outside of school. She needs professional help."

"She's improving," I said. "Every day she's better."

Dorothy exhaled, slow. "You're a good man, Matt, and we love you. We know you'll do whatever you have to do for Anna, but you have to see that she needs a stable environment. And since you won't let us lend you the money you need—"

"You don't have the money I need."

"We could always make something work, but that's your business, and I won't argue with you about it anymore. But I also will not back down about Anna. She needs someone now, and we can be there for her."

"I'm here for her."

"I know you believe you are," Dorothy said. "But is it true?"

Once again, a rolling wave of anger swept through me, forcing its way to the surface. This time it hit with such force that there was no chance of keeping it inside.

From that point on, the conversation turned bad.

Eventually, I slammed the phone down and pushed away from the table. I walked to the window and looked out at Anna in the yard. She didn't see me at first, but when she did, she waved and pointed to her snowman. It was a sad, brown thing, almost as tall as her, but the excitement on her face shone bright and broke inside me.

Are you still having the nightmares?

I turned away from the window and sat back at the table. There was a stack of unpaid bills on the counter. I grabbed them and started flipping through, one by one. My plan was to get my mind off my conversation with Dorothy, but of course it just made things worse.

Are you still having the nightmares?

I got up and paced the small kitchen, going over everything Dorothy had said. She'd been right about one thing. Anna did need special attention, and maybe I wasn't in the best position to provide it for her, but that didn't mean things wouldn't get better. And there was one thing Dorothy was overlooking.

Anna was my daughter.

It was in her best interest to stay with me, not to be pawned off every time things got tough. If I hadn't let her go after Beth died, when I didn't know how I was going to make it through my days, then I sure as hell wasn't going to let her go now.

I reached for the attorney's letter and went over it again. This time the anger faded as I read, replaced with absolute calm and one single thought: Anna and I had been through worse, a hell of a lot worse, and we'd survived.

If Dorothy and Jerry thought I'd hand her over without a fight, they were in for a shock.

Outside, Dash started barking, loud and urgent.

I figured one of the alley cats had wandered into our yard, but then I heard Anna's voice.

"Daddy!"

I dropped the letter on the table and crossed the kitchen to the window and looked out.

There was a man in my yard.

He was wearing a black snow cap and a dark blue pea-coat. His back was to me, and he was leaning over Anna, covering her like a shadow while Dash snapped at his heels.

"Daddy!"

I ran to the door and pushed it open right as Anna was coming up the steps.

The man followed behind her.

"Someone's here for you," she said.

The man stopped at the bottom of the stairs. His face was partially hidden by the cap, and it took a second for me to recognize him.

"Jesus, Jay."

"What?" Jay laughed and slid the snow cap off. "I told you I'd be back."

8

Jay sat at the kitchen table, and I handed him a cup of coffee. He held it with both hands and nodded toward the window. "She's gotten big."

"That's what they do."

"I guess so," he said. "Still strange to see."

I sat across from him and watched him drink. It'd been a couple weeks since that night in the bar, and from the way he looked, I didn't think he'd slept much since. His skin was gray, and his eyes were flat and rimmed heavy and dark. Looking at him was like looking at a skull.

If I'd had any doubts about Jay using again, they were gone now.

I watched him and waited for him to say something.

I didn't wait long.

"You didn't expect to see me?"

"I didn't think about it," I said. "But I'm not all that surprised, either."

"Well, here I am." He set the coffee cup on the table and leaned back. "Came to get your answer."

"My answer?" I shook my head. "Christ, Jay. Don't start with that shit again."

"Now's the time to act," Jay said. "Roach told me the woman has her appointment this week."

"I already gave you my answer. Nothing's changed."

Jay reached for his cup, frowned. "Don't do that."

"Do what?"

"Pretend like you're above it all." He took a sip and winced. "I mean, who the fuck do you think you're talking to? I know you, Matt."

"You *knew* me," I said. "People change."

"Let's cut the bullshit. I know what happened to you, and I know all about your situation."

"You checked up on me?"

"Something was different with you," he said. "I knew about Beth, but I could tell there was more. Now I know."

"You don't know anything."

Jay sat forward and ran one finger along the rim of his cup. "I know you came home from the desert with a few loose screws rattling around in your head."

I looked up fast—too fast.

Jay didn't seem to notice.

"I know the plant closed and now you're flat broke. I know you had to mortgage the house to cover your little girl's medical bills after the accident, not to mention Beth's funeral." He stared at me. "I know you're in a hole that you won't be able to climb out of anytime soon."

"That's enough."

"I still can't believe you borrowed money from Brian, or that you haven't paid him back yet."

"Jay—"

"I can only think of one reason why you'd do something that fucking stupid." He paused, pointed at me. "You're more desperate than I thought."

"Are you done?"

"You need this job, whether you admit it or not."

"Not bad enough to do what you're asking."

Jay folded his arms over his chest. "I only need you to drive, Matt." He frowned. "You still have your van, right? Didn't sell it?"

"The answer's no."

"We're talking a few hours of your time, tops. Just long enough for me to call and arrange the exchange with the old man. Once we have the money, the wife goes home safe, and we split the cash."

"No."

"Do you have a choice?" Jay hesitated. "What do you think is going to happen with Murphy if you don't pay him?"

"He won't come after me."

"No, but if word gets back to the Vogler brothers—"

"I'll deal with that when it's an issue."

"It's already an issue, Matt. That's what I'm trying to tell you. It's now or never."

I listened to Jay and didn't say anything else. He was repeating himself, and eventually I started blocking him out. Soon, all I could focus on was how he moved in his chair, shifting his weight like he was sitting on knives.

"What's wrong with you?" I asked.

Jay stopped talking. "What?"

"Look at you." I pointed at him. "You're using again."

"It's the flu. I'm still a little shaky."

I laughed. "You don't have the Goddamn flu."

Jay looked past me to the window, then down at his hands. "It's under control, Matt."

"You expect me to risk everything on your word? What happens when you fuck up?"

"I'm not going to fuck up."

"You always fuck up," I said. "All kinds of things can go wrong. You being a junkie only adds to the list."

Jay finished the last of his coffee and stood up. "Roach found a warehouse down by the river. Some artist used it as a studio, but he disappeared a while ago, and now the place is deserted. We're going down tomorrow to check it out." He took a pen from his pocket and a napkin from the table and wrote a number on the back. "I'm staying at her place. If you change your mind, call."

He held the napkin out to me, but I didn't take it.

"I can work something out with Murphy and the Vogler brothers," I said. "I'm not desperate."

"As far as I'm concerned, we're all desperate." He dropped the napkin on the table in front of me and tapped it with one finger. "Call me."

I stayed at the table and watched him walk out the front door. I heard Dash bark, then Jay tell Anna her snowman looked great. She thanked him, but there was no warmth in her voice.

I got up and stood at the window and watched as Jay closed the gate and walked down the street, out of sight.

• • •

That night I made Anna's favorite meal, macaroni and cheese mixed with a can of baby snow peas. I sat across from her and watched her work her way through two helpings.

Halfway through the second, she looked up at me and frowned. "Why aren't you eating?"

"Not hungry," I said. "I'll eat later."

Anna lifted her fork and took another bite, chewing slowly. For an instant, she looked so much like Beth that I forgot to breathe. It wasn't just a gesture, or the way she tilted her head in the kitchen light, it was everything, and it was like watching a fading memory.

"Who was that man today?"

I was still thinking about Beth, and it took a minute for me to come back. "What man?"

Anna's shoulders sagged. "He was here this afternoon."

I closed my eyes, nodded. "Right, sorry."

"Who was he?"

"An old friend."

"I didn't like him."

I eased back in my chair. "Why not?"

"He tried to kick Dash."

"He did *what*?"

"Dash bit one of his shoes, and he tried to kick him." She looked up at me, and I saw a dark light burning behind her eyes. "Dash is just a dog. He doesn't know any better. He was trying to protect me."

"Don't worry about him," I said. "You won't have to see him again. He's not coming back."

"Good."

Anna didn't say anything else. She turned back to her food, and it didn't take long for her to finish.

"Can I be excused?"

I pointed to her plate. "Clean up."

She carried her dishes to the sink, and I watched her wash them and put them in the dish rack to dry. The entire time, all I could think about was who she was going to be in a few years. What kind of life would she have if things didn't change? What kind of future was I giving her?

For the first time, I let myself wonder if Jerry and Dorothy were right. Anna was young, and I could still protect her, but in a few years she was going to be a teenager with a life of her own.

What then?

I thought about Beth and late night conversations about our future, and how a run down house on the south side was never part of our long term plans.

We'd always assumed that things would change and we'd be able to give Anna so much more. And why not? We were just starting out at the time, our family was new, and things would only get better.

That's what we believed.

Anna finished washing her dishes, and I called her over. I held out my arms and pulled her close. She hugged me back at first, then she dropped her arms to her sides and made a small choking sound.

"Daddy, I can't breathe."

I let her go. "Sorry, sweetheart."

"Hugs shouldn't hurt," she said. "Don't you know that?"

I told her I did, then I watched her walk out of the kitchen. She called for Dash, and the two of them ran down the hall and disappeared into her room and closed the door.

I stayed at the table for a while longer, thinking about Anna, the future, and that she'd been right.

Hugs shouldn't hurt.

But sometimes, they still did.

9

It was impossible to sleep.

I stayed in bed for as long as I could, staring up at the faded brown water stains on the ceiling, and turning the situation with Jay over in my mind. After a while, it got to be too much, and I pushed the sheets away and sat up.

The clock by my bed read 2:17 a.m.

I walked through the dark to the kitchen and opened the cabinet by the sink. There was a half-empty bottle of Jameson inside that I kept for nights like this one.

I grabbed the bottle and a blue plastic Minnie Mouse cup from the dish drainer and poured myself a drink.

I downed it in two swallows.

The burn rose in my throat, screamed through my sinuses, and cleared the fog from my head. I leaned back against the counter, feeling the warmth spread across my chest and down my arms, then I poured another.

This time, I drank slow.

Once it was gone, I rinsed the cup and set it in the sink. I grabbed the bottle and the phone and walked out to the living room and sat on the couch. The napkin with Jay's number was on the coffee table. I picked it up and ran my fingers over the thin black numbers scratched onto the surface and tried to think of another way, any other way, but nothing came to me.

I lifted the bottle and took a drink, then I picked up the phone and dialed. I let it ring several times before hanging up and trying again.

This time Rochelle answered.

It was the first time I'd heard her voice in years, and I was amazed at how little it'd changed.

"Hey, Roach."

She was quiet for a moment, then she sighed and said, "You have any idea what time it is?"

I told her I did, then asked for Jay.

She grunted and handed the phone over. When Jay came on the line, his voice was tired and angry. I didn't blame him, but I also didn't care.

"I need to know something," I said.

"What time is it?"

"I have to know that you and I are on the same page."

"The what?"

"If something goes wrong, I want us to have a plan."

Jay coughed. "Hold on a minute."

He shuffled something around on the other end of the line. Then I heard the scrape of a cigarette lighter and a long inhale. "Okay, start over."

"We don't hurt anyone," I said. "No matter what."

"No one is going to get hurt."

"A lot can happen if things fall apart."

Jay paused. "Is this really why you called?"

"It's important to me."

"I can see that." Another long inhale. "Okay, no one gets hurt, you have my word."

"Even if he doesn't pay."

"He'll pay."

The smugness in his voice grated on me, but I ignored it. "But if he doesn't, we walk. Do you agree?"

"Is this what's holding you back?"

I thought about the question and my answer. There were a lot of reasons to back out, but every time I tried, all I saw was Anna slipping away from me, one step at a time.

"Yeah," I said. "It is."

"Then I give you my word. No one gets hurt, whether we get the money or not."

"Okay."

"Okay?" Jay hesitated. "Does this mean you're in?"

"I guess it does."

Jay laughed. The sound was so natural and so bright that it almost made me smile.

"It's about time you came around," he said. "A chance like this doesn't pop up every day."

We talked for a while longer, and I listened to him go over a few details of his plan. Every time I said anything, my voice seemed to trail off, far and distant, like it was coming from someone else.

"We're going this Friday," Jay said. "That gives us almost a week to get ready."

"Friday?"

I wanted to tell him that it was too soon, but I didn't. This Friday or Friday next year, it didn't matter. It was never going to be the right time.

"Roach is working that day," Jay said. "We'll park down the street and she'll call when the woman is leaving. Then we'll move in."

"Witnesses?"

"There aren't many people outside. As long as we move fast, no one should notice us."

I asked him about the warehouse and told him I wanted to drive the route a few times before Friday.

He agreed, said, "You're sure you're in? I don't want you backing out at the last minute."

"I'm not backing out."

Jay exhaled into the phone. "I don't want you to worry about anything. Like I said, all you do is drive. I'll handle the rest."

"Remember what we talked about. If—"

"No one is going to get hurt, Matt." He laughed to himself. "Shit, we won't even have guns. That has to make you feel a little better."

I thought about it, and he was right, it did.

"Your entire life is about to change for the better, my friend. I'm telling you, you made the right choice."

I listened and did my best to believe him.

• • •

After I hung up, I leaned back on the couch and thought about Jay's plan. He'd done his homework. He'd learned the woman's routine, and he knew where she would be and when. He'd scoped out the location, and marked the best route in and out of the area.

It was risky, but it could work.

If it did, I'd be able to take Anna out of the city. She'd grow up in a good area and have the life Beth and I always wanted her to have. That alone would be worth the risk.

But if it didn't work?

I pushed the thought away. I knew if I started focusing on everything that could go wrong, I'd be lost. I had to believe it would all come out the way I wanted it to or it would be over.

I still had my eyes closed when I heard the hinges on Anna's door creak open, followed by the rapid click of small claws on the wood floors.

I opened my eyes in time to see Dash crossing through the living room toward the kitchen. I listened to him take a long, sloppy drink from his bowl before starting back.

As he passed, I said, "Hello, Dash."

Dash didn't stop or slow down, just growled and disappeared back into Anna's room.

I reached for the Jameson bottle on the coffee table and walked over to the window and looked out at the darkness. There was a light on across the street at Carrie's house, and I stared at it for a long time.

Something about it made me feel better, less alone.

I'd have to talk to her tomorrow, tell her I picked up a weekend shift and ask her to watch Anna. I hated to lie to her, but I didn't see any other way.

When all of this was over, when I'd squared up with Murphy and moved away from Jerry and Dorothy, when Anna was safe and happy, then maybe I'd tell Carrie the truth. I'd explain what I did, and that I did it because I couldn't see any other way out.

She'd be mad, but she'd understand.

I hoped.

I stood there for a while longer, staring out at the light coming from her window and wishing she'd walk by. I knew if I saw her, even briefly, it would be enough for me to sleep.

But I didn't see her.

And sleep never came.

PART II

1 0

The phone rang at exactly three o'clock.

Jay picked it up, listened, said, "Okay." Then he flipped the phone shut and reached for the black gym bag on the floor by his feet. "She's there."

"How much time do we have?"

"About an hour." He unzipped the bag and started filling it with the items from the coffee table: black pillowcase, ski masks, duct tape, handcuffs. "We'll head over now and wait."

I nodded and tried to seem calm, but inside I could feel the tension building. I used to feel the same way before night patrols, but back then I welcomed the feeling. I saw it as a reminder to be careful, to be sharp, and to be safe. But this was different.

This time, it felt like a warning.

I leaned forward and looked down at my wedding ring. It felt loose on my finger, and I spun it around two or three times, silently reminding myself why I was here.

"You still with me, Matt?" Jay looked at me, smiled. "Are you having second thoughts?"

"Of course I am."

"In a few hours it'll all be over," Jay said. "This is the easy part."

"The easy part?"

"All we have to do is stay focused and stick to the plan. If we do that, all the little pieces will fall into place, and you'll be back home to that little girl before she wakes up in the morning."

I looked away and didn't say anything.

"Come on." Jay stood and slid the gym bag over his shoulder. "Let's get it over with."

I glanced at my ring and spun it one more time, then I got up and followed Jay out of the apartment and down the stairs toward the street and whatever came next.

• • •

When we got to the salon, Jay and I circled the block twice, looking for anything that seemed out of place. Then we parked down the street where we had a clear view of the front, and we waited.

The sky was thin and gray, and the wind was sharp. The few shoppers we saw on the street all walked by with their heads down, shielding themselves from the wind.

It all looked exactly how Jay said it would.

I tapped my fingers against the steering wheel and scanned the road. There was a black Town Car parked in the lot across the street, and I pointed it out.

"Do you think that's hers?"

Jay looked up, nodded. "Has to be."

There was an older man sitting in the driver's seat. He had a newspaper open over the steering wheel in front of him.

"Someone's inside," I said.

Jay squinted. "She must have a driver."

"You didn't say anything about a driver."

"Does it matter?"

"Does it matter?" I bit down hard and tried to keep my voice calm. "He's unaccounted for, so, yes, it matters."

Jay shook his head. "We'll be gone before he notices. Don't worry."

"He's a witness," I said. "It doesn't matter how fast we move. Eventually he's going to notice she's gone, and he'll go to the cops."

Jay leaned back and stared at me. "Do you want to back out, Matt? Is that what this is?"

I thought about it. I could even feel the words form in my throat, but they wouldn't come. If I called it off, we'd have to wait another two weeks before we could try again, and even then, we'd still have to deal with the driver.

Besides, a lot could happen in two weeks.

Jerry and Dorothy wouldn't be a problem. I could hold them and their attorney off for a while, but Murphy would be different. I'd known him for a long time, and he was only patient up to a point. Sooner or later, he was going to get angry, and when he did, things would turn bad in a hurry. I'd seen it happen too many times not to let it worry me.

"What's it going to be?"

"We'll stick to the plan," I said. "But it has to be quick. No fucking around."

"You got it."

"I mean it, Jay. I want to be gone before he knows anything is happening."

"I'll be a blur," Jay said. "You'll see."

Jay smiled, and I turned away.

He was trying to lighten the mood, but seeing that wide grin of his made me want to put my fist through it. I didn't know if that would make me feel better or not, but I had a feeling it might.

Neither of us said anything else, and time passed.

After a while, I started to get nervous.

I looked at my watch. "It's been over an hour."

"She'll be out when she's out." Jay reached into his pocket and took out the cell phone and set it on the dashboard. "Roach will call when it's time, so relax."

Relax?

There were a lot of things I could've said, but it wasn't worth the hassle, so I kept my mouth shut. A minute later, the cell phone rang, vibrating loud against the dashboard.

We both sat up fast.

Jay grabbed the phone. He checked the number, flipped it open, and put it to his ear. He listened without saying a word then hung up and said, "It's time."

I started the engine.

Jay climbed into the back and unzipped the gym bag. He took out the ski masks, handed one to me, and we slipped them over our heads.

"Okay," he said. "Let's go."

I checked my mirror then pulled out onto the street. Jay moved over and crouched next to the sliding side door, one hand on the handle, ready to move.

I drove slow, watching the front of the salon the entire time. Once the door opened, I sped up and stopped hard out front.

The woman who walked out looked to be in her fifties, younger than I'd expected. She had dyed black hair covered by a gold scarf, and she wore a long red coat with a fur collar turned up against the wind.

She crossed the sidewalk toward the street and didn't seem to notice the van until Jay opened the door and jumped out.

Then I heard her yell.

I looked over at the Town Car parked across the street. The driver was still inside, and the newspaper was still open in front of him, but he wasn't reading it anymore. He was watching us.

When he noticed the mask, I saw the understanding pass over his face like a shadow. He fumbled with the paper, tossing it aside, and opened the door.

"We've got to go," I said.

I looked over at Jay. He had the woman by one arm, pulling her toward the van. She didn't scream or call for help. Instead, she reached into her purse and took out a red tube of pepper spray.

I started to warn him, but Jay saw it in time. He grabbed her arm before she could use it.

Across the street, the driver was out of the car.

"Now," I said. "We have to move now."

Jay took the pepper spray from the woman and dragged her off the curb, toward the van. This time, she turned with the momentum and swung her purse, hard. It connected with the side of Jay's head, and I saw his knees buckle under him.

For an instant, I thought he was going to go down, but it didn't happen. Somehow, he steadied himself. He let go of the woman's coat, bent down, and grabbed her around the waist, lifting her off her feet and throwing her into the van.

She landed hard.

Jay climbed in after her. "Go!"

As we pulled away, the driver ran after us, reaching out, screaming for us to stop. I watched him in the mirror, standing alone in the street with his hands on top of his head, watching us go.

• • •

The highway was only a few blocks away. I could feel the adrenaline buzzing through me, and I had to force myself to drive the speed limit. I didn't see any cops, and I didn't think anyone was following us, but my heart was beating so hard that my chest ached.

I tried to focus on my breathing, deep and slow, and did my best to stay calm.

It helped a little.

Behind me, I heard the familiar click of handcuffs, and I looked back. The woman was sitting on the floor of the van with her head down. Her coat was bunched up around her waist, and there was a wide tear across one shoulder.

One of her shoes was missing.

Whatever fight she'd had in her outside the salon, it was gone now. Seeing her broken like that touched something raw and painful inside me, and I didn't like it.

"Don't be scared," I said. "We're not going to—"

"Hey!" Jay hit the back of my seat. "Shut the fuck up."

"I was just—"

"Don't talk to her."

I started to say something else, but I stopped before I got started. Jay was right. I didn't like it, but it was probably better for all of us if we didn't talk to her.

I glanced down at the speedometer and concentrated on my driving while Jay took the black pillowcase from the gym bag and started to slip it over the woman's head.

Before he could, she spoke, her voice small but steady.

"I'm not scared," she said. "Not of you."

I looked back.

The woman's hair had come undone and fallen forward, covering half of her face, but I could still see her eyes, bright and focused. Then, as Jay slid the pillowcase over her head, she smiled at me.

The look was cold, empty, and totally unafraid.

Once her head was covered, I pulled off my ski mask. I could hear Jay tearing off strips of duct tape to keep the pillowcase in place, but I didn't turn to look. Instead, I stared straight out and kept my eyes locked on the road ahead.

That smile.

I never wanted to see it again.

11

Twenty minutes later, we passed through the gates and drove down the long dirt road leading to the storage docks by the river. I pulled in alongside the building and shut off the engine.

"We're here."

I looked back at Jay. He was sitting across from the woman, leaning against the side of the van with his head back and his eyes closed. There was sweat on his face, and his skin looked pale and rough.

"You ready?"

Jay pushed himself over to the sliding door and reached for the handle. There was a dark bruise forming on the side of his head, and I asked if he was okay.

Jay ignored the question and pulled the door open. I walked around to the side of the van to meet him, and we each took one of the woman's arms and helped her out.

She didn't struggle, and she didn't speak.

Jay led us across the parking lot to a thick metal door on the side of the far storage dock. He pulled a key from his pocket, but his hands were shaking, and it took a minute before he was able to slide it into the lock and open the door.

Inside was a long, dark hallway lined with broken bricks and exposed pipes, all covered in a thick layer of dirt. The air was damp and smelled like turpentine and rotted wood.

After I'd agreed to do the job, I'd made several practice runs, driving from the salon to the warehouse, but I never saw the inside. Now I wished I had.

Jay must've seen it on my face, because he held up one hand and said, "Don't worry, it gets better."

I nodded and held the woman's arm as I helped her through the door. A few steps in, her foot hit one of the loose bricks, and she stumbled.

I caught her before she fell. "I've got you."

The woman turned to the sound of my voice, and I could hear her breathing through the pillowcase. Once again, I felt the urge to tell her that everything was fine, and that no one was going to hurt her, but this time I kept quiet and led her down the hall toward another door where Jay was waiting.

He unlocked the second door, and we followed him inside.

The main room was nicer than the hallway, but not by much. There were stacks of plywood along the wall, and a metal desk in the corner. The floor was covered with dust and heavy splashes of paint and wood stain. Along the top of the walls, just below the ceiling, was a row of small square windows. The glass was caked with dirt, and the light slanting through into the room was the color of rust.

Jay pointed to a red metal chair in the far corner next to an exposed pipe. "Put her over there."

I led the woman to the chair and helped her sit. Jay knelt behind her and unlocked one of her wrists. He took the open cuff and secured it to the pipe.

"Did you get her purse?" he asked.

"Still in the van, I think."

Jay pushed himself up, slow. He walked outside and came back a minute later with her purse. He set it on the desk and opened it.

I stood next to him. "Are you doing okay?"

"That bitch almost killed me."

"No, she didn't," I said. "Besides, we made it."

"Yeah." He started digging through her purse. "But I still need a fucking drink."

"First we make the call," I said. "I want to get this over with."

"We have to wait for Roach."

"Why?"

Jay glanced back at the woman, then leaned in close and whispered. "She's staying at the salon in case the police have questions. Once it's all clear, she'll meet us here and then we'll call the old man and set up the exchange."

"How long?"

"However long it takes." Jay took the woman's wallet from her purse and pulled out several bills. He counted them and slid them into his pocket. "Did she have anything else on her?"

"I didn't check."

"Maybe you should."

"What happened to just driving?"

Jay looked at me. "You want me to do it?"

He dropped the wallet back in her purse and started toward her, but I stopped him.

"Forget it," I said. "I'll do it."

I walked back to where the woman was sitting and knelt beside her. I checked her pockets, all empty.

Before I got up, I asked her if she needed anything.

Silence.

I started to ask her again, but then I heard an engine and the sound of tires passing over the gravel lot outside.

I got up and looked over at Jay.

He nodded and put a finger to his lips.

A minute later, a car door slammed.

I walked over to where he was standing and said, "Who is that?"

Jay shook his head and opened the top desk drawer. There was a black .38 inside. He picked it up.

I wasn't expecting the gun, and it took an instant to register what I was seeing. Once I did, I grabbed his arm and said, "You told me no guns."

"First this." Jay nodded toward the door. "Then we'll talk."

I stepped closer. "Put it back."

"This isn't the time to—"

Someone knocked.

For a moment, neither of us moved. Then I started for the door.

"Wait," Jay said. "Don't answer it."

I ignored him. I knew if the police had found us, the last thing they'd do was knock.

Jay followed me to the door.

I leaned in close and said, "Who is it?"

A tiny voice. "Open the Goddamn door."

I reached for the handle and pulled.

Rochelle stepped inside, rubbing her hands over her arms. "What the hell is wrong with you two? Don't leave me standing out there like that."

Her dark hair was tucked behind her ears, and she was wearing a thin, silver coat and skirt that ended closer to her waist than her knees. When I looked, I saw that the skin on her legs was almost blue.

"Next time get dressed before you go outside."

"Are you being funny, Matt?" Rochelle's eyes narrowed. "That's not like you."

I turned toward Jay and pointed at the gun. "You want to explain? I thought we talked about this."

Jay lowered the gun, never taking his eyes off Roach. "You're not supposed to be here. What about the cops?"

"They didn't show." She walked past us into the main room. When she saw the woman in the corner, she turned back and spoke softly. "The driver made a call, then drove away. I stuck around for twenty minutes then told everyone I felt sick and needed to go home. I don't think anyone saw a thing."

Jay smiled at me, and I could see the relief in his eyes. "Did I tell you?"

"What about the driver?" I asked. "Did he follow us?"

"He went east into town." She pointed to the woman's purse on the desk and looked at Jay. "Did you check?"

Jay nodded.

"How much?"

Jay reached into his pocket and handed her the money he'd pulled from the woman's purse. Rochelle's lips moved as she counted it. When she finished, she put her arms around his neck and whispered something to him that I couldn't hear.

"Just hurry," he said.

Roach folded the money and slid it into her jacket pocket. "I'll be back before you know it."

She started for the door.

"Wait, we have to finish this."

"Oh, right." Roach reached into her pocket and took out a prepaid cell phone. She tossed it to Jay. "Wait until I get back. Let him stew for a while longer."

"You got it."

Roach blew Jay a kiss then walked out.

Once she was gone, I turned to him.

"Where is she going?"

"Don't worry about it."

"Are you kidding?" I backed up, paced the room. "I hate secrets, Jay. You lied about the gun, and now this?"

Jay looked down at the gun as if seeing it for the first time. Then he opened the top desk drawer and dropped it inside. "I have it for emergencies."

I stood there, watching him, wanting to yell, but I didn't know where to start. I also didn't see the point. I knew what Jay was like before I agreed to do the job, and I knew exactly what I was getting myself into.

There was no one to blame but myself.

Jay leaned against the desk, his shoulders moving with his breath. He didn't look at me, but I knew he could feel me there, staring at him. Still, he didn't say anything for a long time, and when he did, it was another lie.

"Don't worry, Matt. It's all under control."

1 2

After an hour, I looked down at my watch and said, "Where the hell is she?"

"She'll be here."

"He's going to call the police," I said. "If he hasn't already."

"He won't."

"We have to make the call, now."

Jay was sitting at the desk, leaning forward with his head resting on his arms. He didn't say anything.

"Did you hear me?" I asked. "We're running out of time. We've waited long enough."

Jay exhaled long and slow, then pushed himself up and paced the room, ignoring me.

I watched him for a minute, then shook my head and said, "Jesus, look at you."

It was hot in the warehouse, but Jay was shaking. His arms were folded tight in front of his chest, like he was trying to stay warm, and there were tiny beads of sweat on his skin, running down his face.

"I'm fine," he said. "Just cold."

"Goddamn it." I leaned against the workbench. "I knew it."

"I said I'm fine."

I turned and slammed my fist against the top of the bench. The sound was loud, and Jay jumped.

The woman in the corner didn't flinch.

"I'm done waiting," I said. "Give me the phone."

"Hold on." He held up his hands. "We're on schedule. It's just now starting to get dark. We can't do anything until then anyway, so—"

"I can't believe I trusted you," I said. "I knew you'd find a way to fuck this up, but I bought into it anyway."

"Once Roach gets back, we'll make the call. Everything will work out, you'll see."

"She's not coming back."

"She'll be here."

"If you think I'm just going to sit here and wait for the cops to show up, you're out of your mind."

Jay stared at me, his eyes darting back and forth between mine. "You want to make the call?" He reached into his pocket and took out a white business card and held it out. "The phone's on the desk."

"No, you call and I drive. Like we agreed, remember?"

Jay slipped the card into his pocket. "I'm not calling until Roach is back."

I bit down hard on the insides of my cheeks to keep from screaming, then looked over at the old woman. She hadn't moved in a while, but I knew she was listening to every word we said.

I turned to Jay and shook my head. It took every bit of self-control I had to walk away.

"Where are you going?"

I didn't answer, and I didn't look back. I was afraid if I did, if I had to look at Jay's face one more time, I'd end up killing him.

I walked down the hall to the front door and kicked it open. Once outside, the cold wind coming off the river cut through me, clearing my head.

I had a decision to make.

The longer we waited, the more dangerous the situation became. If the driver didn't call the police from the scene, it was safe to assume the cops weren't involved, at least not yet. That meant the old man was expecting a call.

He was waiting, but for how long?

I crossed the lot to the van and leaned against the far side, out of the wind, and cursed myself for not seeing this coming. Every part of me had known signing on with Jay was a bad idea, but I went along anyway. I gambled with my life and my freedom, but worse than that, I gambled with Anna.

If I got caught, I wouldn't see my daughter again until she was an adult, a completely different person. They'd take her childhood from me, and I'd only have myself to blame.

No matter what, I couldn't let that happen.

I stayed outside for a while longer, fighting the urge to climb in the van and drive away. In the end, I decided to stay and make sure the woman was safe. Everything had to go as planned, and if that meant stepping up and taking charge, that's what I was going to do.

When I went back inside, Jay was sitting at the desk, rocking back and forth in the chair. When he saw me, he stood and smiled. "I thought you left."

I took the cell phone off the desk and held out my hand. "Give me the number."

"Roach isn't back yet."

"I'm not waiting."

"This is my call, Matt. Remember, we—"

I stepped closer. "Give me the number or I'll take it from you."

Jay looked up at me but didn't move.

"You know I can do it," I said.

For an instant, I thought he was going to take a swing at me. Part of me hoped he would. My muscles were wound so tight they felt like they were going to snap, and after all that'd happened, it would've been a pleasure to take some of that tension out on him.

But he didn't.

Instead, he reached into his pocket for the card. Before he took it out, he turned toward the door, cocked his head to the side. "Listen."

At first I didn't hear anything, then I did.

Someone was pulling up outside.

"See?" Jay smiled. "I told you."

• • •

Jay met Roach at the door. I stayed by the desk, turning the cell phone over in my hands. I could hear them talking in the hallway, but it was all whispers, and I didn't catch anything.

When they came into the room, Rochelle pushed past me and sat at the desk. She had a brown paper bag in her hand. She opened it and took out a thick blue rubber band and two thin syringes.

"Are you fucking kidding me?" I looked over at Jay. "This is what we've been waiting for?"

Jay was leaning against the wall, his face wet with sweat. Every part of him seemed to tremble.

I crossed the room and pulled him away from the wall, then slammed him back against it again, hard. A thin mist of dust fell around us, and when I let him go, he lost his balance and slipped to the ground.

"Jesus, Matt."

I walked back to the desk. Rochelle was staring at me, and when I got close, she stood and stepped away, her hands out in front of her.

"Don't touch me."

I looked down at Jay. "You told me this wasn't going to be a problem."

"It's not." He stumbled over his words. "I mean it won't be, it isn't—"

"Do you know the kind of shit we'll be in if we're caught? Do you have any idea what's at stake?"

Rochelle laughed.

I turned on her. "This is on you. This has always been on you."

"He's a big boy. He can make his own decisions." She looked me up then down. "When did you get so uptight? I don't remember you being *this* bad."

"Junkies put me on edge."

"Fuck you."

I stepped closer to her then felt Jay's hand on my arm. I shook it off. "Get your hand off me."

He did.

"Come on, Matt. Calm down."

"Give me the number."

Jay looked past me to Roach, then shook his head. "It's too soon. I want him to sweat. I'll call in a few minutes and then we'll—"

I swung, putting all my weight behind the punch, and connected just beneath Jay's ribs. I felt something give, and he dropped, struggling for breath.

Roach closed on me, slapping me, screaming.

"Don't fucking touch him."

I put my hand on her chest and pushed her away. She hit the desk chair, tripped, and fell backward, hitting the ground hard. She stayed there, staring up at me.

I bent down and started digging through Jay's pockets until I found the business card with the old man's number.

Jay moved to his knees, still struggling to breathe.

I stood over him. "Once this is done, you and I are through. I don't want to see you or hear from you again."

"Matt—"

I reached down and opened the top desk drawer and took out the .38. I pointed it at the brown paper bag.

"When I come back, that shit better be gone. If it's still here, I'll throw it out myself."

Roach pushed herself to her feet and said, "Who the fuck do you think you are? You're not—"

I lifted the gun and pointed it at her head.

She screamed and backed up against the wall, staring down at the floor. "Okay, okay."

"From here on, we're going to do this my way," I said. "Now get rid of it. All of it."

This time, they both kept quiet.

I lowered the gun and headed for the door. As I walked out, I heard Roach yell after me.

"You're still an asshole, Matt. You know that?"

I didn't say anything, I didn't need to.

She was right.

1 3

Outside, the snow had started to fall, and the wind came off the river in sharp, freezing gusts. I pulled my coat tight as I crossed the gravel lot to my van. I got in and tossed the gun into the glove compartment. Then I started the engine and turned on the heat.

My hands were shaking from the adrenaline, and I squeezed them together tight. I could feel the tension racing through me, and I slammed my fist against the steering wheel again and again, trying to let it out.

It didn't work.

Every bad thing I knew about Jay had shown itself. I'd hoped he was different since coming out of prison. But he wasn't, and now it was up to me to do damage control.

If there was a way to fix the situation, I couldn't see it, and the more I thought about it, the worse it all seemed. I couldn't take the woman home, and I couldn't walk away and leave her with Roach and Jay.

I was stuck.

I knew I had to make sure she was safe, and that meant everything from here on had to go as planned. The only way out that I could see was to keep moving forward.

I had to make the call.

But first, I needed to calm down.

I leaned back in the seat and counted each breath, trying to clear my head. Outside, there was a long line of cottonwood trees stretching along the road leading down to the river. Their branches were stripped bare by the season, and they stood, black and cold, silhouetted against the white sky like deep cracks in the surface of the world.

I stared at them for a long time.

Eventually I felt my muscles begin to relax, and soon the world slipped back into focus.

I took the phone from my pocket and looked down at the number on the back of the business card. I knew I had to call, but I didn't know what I was going to say.

Jay had put everything together. He had a location for the drop all set to go. It was a seldom-used bus stop on Fourteenth and Carmine. It seemed like a risky spot to me, but he'd insisted. He said he'd checked it out several times, and it was perfect.

I felt like a fool for trusting his opinion after all that had happened, but we were in too deep now.

Besides, I didn't have a better idea.

I opened the phone and dialed the number. I paused at the end and took a deep breath, trying again to steady myself. Then I hit the Call button.

The phone rang twice.

The man who answered didn't say anything at first. He just breathed into the phone, slow and steady.

Then he said, "Has she been harmed?"

It was an obvious question, but for some reason it stopped me cold. He had a faint accent that I couldn't quite place, and I wondered if this was really the same old man Jay and I had watched on TV that night in the bar.

"Not yet," I said. "But that depends on you."

"Where is she?"

"She's safe, but if you want her back, you need to do exactly what I say."

Silence.

"Put five hundred thousand dollars in a bag and take it to the bus stop on the corner of Fourteenth and Carmine in one hour. Put the bag under the bench and wait for the number eleven bus. When it arrives, leave the bag and get on."

I asked if he understood, but the only sound I heard was his breathing.

"I don't think I have to tell you to come alone," I said. "Or what will happen to her if the police become involved."

The breathing stopped.

"I do not involve the police in my personal affairs."

"That's good," I said. "If you do exactly what I've asked you to do, I'll call again in a couple hours and let you know where you can pick up your wife."

"I won't be the one coming," he said. "Someone else will be there in my place."

"As long as they bring the money, I don't care."

The man hesitated, then said, "One hour."

The line went dead.

I lowered the phone and flipped it shut and stared at the snow swirling outside the window. After a while, I started to imagine what the old man was thinking, the pain he must be feeling, what he was going through.

All because of me.

I tried my best to push these thoughts away, but it was too late. I couldn't do it. My chest felt tight, and my mouth was dry and tasted bitter. I swallowed hard, hoping it would go away, but it didn't.

I stayed in the van for a while longer before getting out and walking back across the parking lot to the warehouse.

The snow was falling heavier now, carried sideways by the wind coming up off the river. I kept my head down until I got to the door, then I reached for the handle and pulled.

It was locked.

"You motherf—" I knocked, loud, hitting the door with the side of my fist. "Jay?"

No one came, so I knocked again, harder this time.

A minute later, I heard someone slide the bolt. I grabbed the handle and yanked the door open.

Roach was standing in the doorway.

"Why the hell did you lock the d—"

Roach grabbed my arm and tried to drag me inside. I pulled away, then I noticed the look on her face.

Roach's eyes were wide, frantic. There were tears on her cheeks, and her entire body seemed to tremble.

"What's wrong?"

"Oh, God, Matt, you have to help me." She inhaled sharp. "He's not breathing."

1 4

At first the words didn't cut through. I heard what she was saying, but the meaning was lost. It didn't make sense. All I could do was push past her and walk down the hall and into the main room.

The woman was still in the corner, handcuffed to the pipe, pillowcase over her head.

Jay was a few feet away, lying on the floor by the desk. He had one arm up over his head, and the other was pinned under him. His eyes were open, staring up at the ceiling, and there was vomit around his mouth and on the front of his jacket.

His lips were blue.

"Oh, Christ."

I ran over and dropped to my knees. I put my head to his chest and listened, but there was no sound. I rolled him onto his side then forced his mouth open and stuck my fingers down as far as they'd go, feeling for anything that might be blocking his air.

I saw Roach come up slow.

"What the hell happened to him?"

"I don't know." Roach folded her arms over her chest. "I swear I don't know."

Her voice was too high, too fast. She was panicking, and unless she calmed down, things were going to get worse.

"Just calm down," I said. "Tell me what happened."

Roach didn't answer, just stared at him.

"Rochelle?"

She looked at me. "I told him it was too much, but he didn't listen. He said we had to get rid of it before you came back, that you'd—"

"Goddamn it." I pulled Jay up to sitting and slapped his face, hard, calling his name. "Wake up!"

Nothing.

"This is your fault," Roach said through tears. "You told him to get rid of it. You said—"

"Jay!" I shook him, not liking the way his head rolled, heavy and loose on his shoulders. Eventually, I eased him back to the floor and felt his neck for a pulse.

I didn't find one.

I closed my eyes and sat on the ground beside him.

Roach watched me, and when I looked up at her, she shook her head and backed away.

I knew what was coming.

"Don't." I pushed myself up and moved closer to her. "I can't have you losing it, not right now."

Roach didn't look at me, and I'm not sure she heard me at all. Whatever was going on in her head, it didn't have anything to do with me.

"He can't be dead," she said. "Do something."

"I can't. He's gone."

"No." Roach backed away. "He can't be dead. He can't be."

Behind us, the woman giggled, bright and childish.

Roach turned on her fast, crossing the room to where she was sitting. I tried to grab her, but she pulled away, never slowing, never taking her eyes off the woman.

When she got close, she reached for the pillowcase, ripped it away, and slapped the woman, hard. "Shut up!"

The woman stopped laughing.

Roach raised her arm to hit her again, but I grabbed her and pulled her back. Roach fought, but I didn't let go.

"Fuck you, Matt! This is your fault. Your fault!"

I pushed Roach away and looked down at the woman.

The left side of her face was bright red, and there was a thin line of blood at the corner of her mouth. I watched as she reached up and touched the blood with her fingertip. She looked at it, then up at me, her eyes bright and clear.

I dragged Roach out of the room and into the hall. She fought me every step, and when I finally got to the door, I kicked it open and pushed her out into the cold.

"What the hell is wrong with you?"

"She's laughing at us. Jay's dead, and she was laughing."

I stood in the doorway, unable to stand still. "Now she's seen our faces."

"Our faces?" Roach stared at me, a mix of hatred and confusion in her eyes. "Jay is dead."

"She can ID us now," I said. "Because of you."

Roach stepped back, shook her head. "It doesn't matter, not anymore." She turned and started walking toward her car. "It's all over."

"Where are you going?" I asked. "What about her?"

"You're in charge now, right? You do what you want."

I thought about going after her, but I didn't. There was no point. Instead, I stayed in the doorway, feeling the cold air rush past me into the room. I watched Roach climb into her car and pull away, leaving me alone.

• • •

The woman was sitting with her legs crossed at the knee, leaning against the armrest of the chair. She watched me as I came in. I didn't say anything to her, and I didn't try to hide my face.

The damage was done.

I walked over to Jay's body and stared down at him. Some people weren't meant to grow old, and Jay had always been one of them. Still, part of me couldn't believe he was gone even though he was lying right in front of me.

I knelt down beside him.

All the color was gone from his skin, and his lips looked blue and swollen. One eye was open, and I reached down and tried to push it closed, but it didn't stay.

I stopped trying and ran through my options.

Thanks to Roach, the woman knew what we looked like. She could ID us, which meant I couldn't let her go, at least not until I had the money. Once the old man paid, I'd have no choice but to take Anna and run.

It wasn't what I'd hoped for, but it was better than prison.

I tried to think of a different way out, but nothing came to me. I had to get the money, which meant I had to stick to Jay's plan. I had no other choice.

I reached down and hooked my arms under Jay's shoulders. I wanted to get him out of the middle of the room, but he was heavier than I'd thought, and it took a while to drag him around the desk and lean him up against the wall.

The woman watched me the entire time.

When I finished, I walked over and asked if I could get her anything.

She stared at me, silent.

I pointed to the bruise forming on the side of her face and said, "I'm sorry that happened."

Again, nothing.

I nodded and turned and started for the door. Before I walked out, I heard her voice, strong and full.

"It's not too late for you."

I looked back. "What?"

She pointed to Jay's body. "You don't have to end up the same way. You still have a chance."

I stared for a moment longer before turning away and walking out. Her words were still in my head when I climbed into the van and started the engine. And by the time I got to the highway, all I felt was sadness.

You still have a chance.

If only that were true.

15

Jay had been right about the drop spot.

Fourteenth and Carmine was surrounded by office buildings. They were all closed for the day, and there were no people on the street. It was quiet, deserted, and accessible from multiple routes.

It was perfect.

I pulled into the parking lot across the street and shut off my headlights. The snow was still falling, and I kept my windshield wipers going while I waited.

The silence was nice, but I couldn't stop thinking about Jay. I knew I had to get him out of my head. If I didn't, if I lost focus and started replaying what had happened, something would go wrong, and I couldn't afford to take that chance.

I looked down at my watch. It'd been an hour since I'd made the call, and there was no sign of anyone.

I tried to ignore the empty feeling building inside me, but it was hard to do.

Something was wrong.

I took the phone from my pocket and flipped it open and found the old man's number. I was about to hit the Call button when I saw a man stumble up Fourteenth Street and turn onto Carmine. When he got to the bus stop, he sat down and began fishing through his pockets. He took out a single cigarette, straightened it, then put it to his lips and lit it with a match.

I watched him shake out the match and drop it on the ground by his feet. Then he inhaled deep and leaned back, stretching out on the bench.

I checked my watch again.

I thought about the old man telling me he wouldn't be the one coming, but I also didn't think this was the guy.

A few minutes later, the number eleven bus pulled up and stopped in front of the bench. No one got off, and when it pulled away, the man was still lying there, staring up at the cold gray sky.

I thought about calling the old man again, but decided against it. Instead, I opened the door and got out and crossed the street to the bus stop.

I approached slowly, keeping an eye out for anyone who might be watching, but the street was empty, and there was no one else around. As I got closer, the man stirred, but he didn't look at me until I was standing at the end of the bench.

When he saw me, he sat up.

"Who the fuck are you?"

There was a loose slur to his voice, and I could smell the wet, spoiled stench of alcohol on his breath.

"Are you the guy?" I asked.

"The guy?"

I looked back over my shoulder at the van and said, "You have something for me?"

"What?" The man tried to push himself up, but his balance wasn't there, and he sat back down. "What the fuck do I have for you? What the hell is wrong with you?"

I backed away, then turned and crossed the street toward my van.

The man on the bench yelled after me. "That's right, motherfucker, I've got something for you, and you better run before I give it to you."

The empty feeling inside me was deeper now, growing black, and I did my best to ignore it. When I got closer to the van, I heard a sound coming from inside.

The phone was ringing.

I ran over and pulled the door open and reached for the phone. The ID read "Unknown Caller." I answered it. The voice on the line was rough and deep, and I recognized it immediately.

"You're late," I said. "You're not taking this situation as seriously as you should."

"That's certainly not the case." The old man's voice was calm, even. "I'm taking this unprovoked attack on my family very seriously. As a matter of fact, it's the only thing I've focused on for the last several hours. You could even say, I've put you at the very top of my priority list."

I didn't say anything. Something wasn't right.

The old man waited for me to speak, then he exhaled into the phone and said, "Are you still there, Mr. Caine?"

Mr. Caine.

Everything inside me fell away and was replaced by a burning panic that filled every part of me, turning the world black. I could feel myself slipping away into that darkness, and I fought it the best I could.

"How—" My voice cracked. "How do you know my name?"

"I know quite a bit about you," the old man said. "And now that we're on more equal ground, I thought we could discuss a renegotiation."

"Renegotiation?"

"The price you're asking," he said. "I believe—"

"How do you know my name?"

"Mr. Caine, I—"

"There is no renegotiation," I said. "This isn't a fucking game."

The old man didn't say anything right away, and I waited. My chest ached, and I could feel my heart slamming against my ribs, making it hard to concentrate.

I forced myself to stay calm.

"No, not a game," the old man said. "Not in any way."

"Then bring the money to the location we discussed." I looked at my watch. "You have fifteen minutes."

"And what about the man on the bench?" he asked. "Do you think he'll be gone by then?"

I leaned forward and scanned the street, looking for any other signs of life. There were no other cars on the block, and the parking lot was empty.

I was alone.

"Where the hell are you? How do you—"

"Mr. Caine, I'm going to make this simple."

"How the fuck do you know my name?"

The old man stopped, sighed, then spoke slowly, as if talking to a child. "There are two hundred fifty-three Chevy cargo vans registered in the metro area. Out of those, only thirty-six are white. Of those thirty-six, thirty-three are registered to private shuttle services or rental companies. That leaves three privately owned."

"You guessed?"

"I don't guess."

"Then, how?"

The old man paused. "Out of those three, Mr. Caine, yours is the only one not currently parked at your house."

Silence.

It took a moment for the words to sink in. When they did, the panic I'd been fighting back broke and ripped through me.

My house.

There were no words.

All at once, the world felt too small, too loud. I wanted to scream, to throw the phone down and run home, but I knew I had to be careful. I had to be smart.

I focused on the windshield wipers sliding back and forth over the glass. I counted each rhythmic pass, grounding myself in the sound. There was a sharp pain building in my head, and my chest burned. I realized I was holding my breath, and I let it out easy.

"My house?"

The old man exhaled, soft, barely a whisper. And when he spoke again, I could almost hear the smile in his voice.

"Now we're starting to understand one another." He paused. "I'd like you to take some time to reexamine the situation, reconsider your position, and then think about how you'd like to proceed."

"What did you—"

The line clicked and went dead.

I sat in the van with the phone pressed hard against my ear, unable to move. There was too much, a mass of swirling thoughts and ideas, and none of them made sense.

Then, behind it all, one thought began to burn through the fog, eclipsing all others until there was nothing else.

He knew where I lived.

1 6

The snow covering the highway was gray and cut through by black tire lines stretching out into darkness. There were hidden patches of ice along the road, and each time I hit one, the van would shift and my heart would climb higher into my throat.

I didn't slow down.

I reached for the phone on the passenger seat and called home. It was the third time I'd tried, and the result was the same.

No answer.

I dropped the phone back on the seat and squeezed the steering wheel so tight my fingers ached. I could feel the tension clawing its way up my spine and worming its way into my brain, making it impossible to think clearly. Once again I tried to tell myself that everything was okay, but the closer I got to home, the less I believed it was true.

When I pulled off the highway and turned onto my street, I could see my house at the end of the block, dark and still. I parked out front and grabbed Jay's gun from the glove compartment then ran up to the front door.

It was locked.

I stepped back and flipped through my keys. My hands were shaking, and it took a minute to find the right one. Once I did, I unlocked the door and went inside.

"Anna?"

The house was dark except for the shadows thrown by the streetlights outside. I hit the switch on the wall, but nothing happened.

The power was out.

Cut?

"Carrie?"

Something moved in the next room. I lifted the gun and followed the sound through the living room to the kitchen.

Carrie was lying on the floor. There was duct tape covering her mouth, and her hands were crossed and bound against her chest. Her eyes were red and swollen, and there was a dark line of dried blood under her nose, running over the tape.

She stared at me, eyes wide, not seeing.

I knelt next to her and pulled the tape from her mouth. She took in several desperate breaths, each one broken by sobs. I grabbed her shoulders and tried to steady her, then I reached up and took her face in my hands.

"Where's Anna?"

Carrie's lips were trembling. She shook her head, said, "I'm so sorry, Matt. I'm so sorry."

"Where is she?" I asked her again, trying my best to keep my voice calm.

Carrie looked up at me, and I saw something change in her eyes. Then the tears came, harder now, running down her cheeks, falling silently into her lap.

I pushed myself up, but my legs felt weak.

I backed out of the kitchen and started toward Anna's room. I could see the shadowed outline of her doorway at the end of the hallway, and I ran down, moving on instinct.

Her door was wide open, and there was a soft, wintry-gray glow leaking in from the windows and casting a half light over the room. I stopped in the doorway and let my eyes adjust to the light, but I already knew.

She was gone.

I stood there, scanning the room from one side to the other, not willing to believe. I could feel the tears pressing behind my eyes, but I held them back.

I didn't want to cry.

I wanted to scream.

The air in the hall felt thin, and the floor started to shift under me. I reached out and put a hand against the door-jamb to steady myself, then I stepped into the room.

The carpet sank wet under my feet.

I looked down.

There was a thick, dark stain spreading out from the doorway into the center of Anna's room. I bent down, slow, and touched it. My fingers came back wet and sticky.

"Oh, God."

This time, the panic screamed up out of the black, and I had no chance of stopping it. I tore through the room, searching closets, checking under the bed, finding nothing.

The room spun.

I sank to my knees at the edge of her bed, staring at the dark stain on the carpet, trying to think. I told myself to focus, but my mind was reeling under a jumble of thoughts, all of them bad, and I couldn't slow them down no matter how hard I tried.

the knife out, then I noticed something wedged between him and the door.

It was a photo.

A Polaroid.

I grabbed the edge and slid the photo out and held it up in the fading gray light.

It was of Anna.

She was sitting on her bed with her hands bent behind her back. She was wearing her pink T-shirt with the stitch of tiny blue flowers across the front, and there was a ring of duct tape wrapped around her head, covering her eyes.

A man was standing next to her, just out of the shot. I could see his hand on her head, grabbing her hair and pulling back, lifting her face up to the camera.

Anna's mouth was open.

She was screaming.

I heard Carrie crying in the kitchen, and I pushed myself up off the floor, never taking my eyes off the wet stain on the carpet.

I moved toward the doorway and stopped.

The door was open into the room, and I could see Anna's handwritten signs taped on the outside. But there was something different about them.

I stepped closer and noticed a dark spot on one of the signs. It was small, wet, and about half the size of a dime. I reached out and pulled the door closed. It was heavier than normal, and I saw why.

Something was pinned to the other side.

At first, I couldn't tell what it was, just a dark shadow hung at eye level. Then I saw the two white spots.

The same but different.

Like snowflakes.

I felt my breath catch, and I stepped back.

The knife was heavy, serrated, and buried to the hilt between Dash's ribs. His head hung loose, his eyes were wide, and his teeth were bared and bloody. There was a long, dark trail under him that ran the length of the door and pooled on the carpet below.

I didn't want to believe what I was seeing, and I turned away.

When I looked back, I saw the scratches. Two sets, like tiny, upturned waning moons sketched into the wood under his paws.

He'd tried to run.

"Oh, Christ, Dash."

He'd tried to run.

I reached out and touched him gently, running my hand over his head and down the back of his neck. I started to pu

17

The old man answered on the third ring.

I started yelling. "If you hurt her, I'll—"

He cut me off. "In one hour, you will deliver my wife to me in Pella Valley."

"Where the fuck is my daughter?"

"You will drive her to the west side of town, past the railroad tracks, where you will find a two-bay car wash next to a white grain silo. You will park on the south side and wait there until I arrive."

"Where is she?"

"Once my wife has been returned, and I am satisfied she has not been harmed, I will release your daughter."

"No," I said. "We do it at the same time. Your wife for my daughter."

"This is not a negotiation, Mr. Caine. My wife will be returned unharmed, and only then will I release your daughter." He paused. "Failure to follow my instructions to the letter will lead to unthinkable consequences. Do you believe me?"

I didn't say anything right away, but something in his voice sent a flood of terror rolling through every part of me, making it hard to breathe.

"I believe you," I said.

"Then you have one hour."

The line clicked, went dead.

I hung up and slid the phone back into my pocket. Then I reached down and picked up the photo of Anna. There was blood on the front, and I wiped it away with my thumb.

Once again, I felt the tears press behind my eyes.

This time, I let them come.

• • •

Carrie watched me as I cut the tape away from her hands. When I finished, she eased herself up and leaned forward, bracing herself against the counter.

I touched her shoulder. "Are you hurt?"

Carrie turned and faced me, her eyes sharp. "Where were you?"

"I—"

"What did you do?"

I shook my head and started to answer, but before I could, Carrie slapped me.

"What did you do?"

She hit me again, but this time I was ready. I grabbed her wrist and stepped behind her, wrapping my arms around hers, holding her still. I could feel her shoulders shake, then there were tears, welling up from some dark place deep inside.

I held her tighter and told her it was okay, that I was going to get Anna back, no matter what.

I told her she had to trust me.

Eventually, the tears stopped, and I felt her fight against my grip. When I let her go, she pushed away from me and sat at the kitchen table with her hands between her knees, rocking back and forth on the chair.

I asked her if she was okay.

"We can't call the police, can we?"

I shook my head. "No."

Carrie stared at me, then down at her hands. "Who were they, Matt?"

I thought about it for a moment, but I didn't have an answer, and I didn't know what to say. In the end, I told her the truth.

"I have no idea."

• • •

Pella Valley was almost thirty miles outside the city. Traffic on the highway was light, but it was still going to be close. If I was going to get there on time, I needed to hurry.

When I got to the river, I turned up the gravel road and followed my headlights through a shatter of snow to the warehouse. I parked out front and ran inside.

The woman watched me as I came in.

I ignored her and went straight for Jay. His skin had turned a rough, grayish blue, and both his eyes were now half-open, clouded and empty.

I tried not to look at him.

I opened his jacket and searched his pockets for the keys to the handcuffs. I found half a pack of American Spirit cigarettes and his black Zippo lighter, but I didn't find his keys.

"Goddamn it."

I started patting him down. I felt the keys in his front pockets, and I took them out and flipped through them as I walked over to where the woman was sitting.

"I'm taking you home."

The woman didn't say anything.

I found the right key and unlocked the cuff from around the pipe. "Do you need anything?"

She stared at me, her eyes moving between mine. "A cigarette?"

I started to tell her I didn't smoke, then I remembered the pack in Jay's jacket. I walked back and took the cigarettes and the lighter from his pocket. There was a piece of yellow legal paper stuck under the pack's cellophane wrapper. I took it out and unfolded it.

The page was covered with notes, all in Jay's scratched handwriting, mostly street names, times, and dates. Along the bottom was a scribbled diagram of the streets surrounding the salon, and on the back were several names and phone numbers and what looked like a grocery list. I ran through the names, not recognizing any of them until I saw mine, then I refolded the paper and slipped it into my pocket.

When all of this was over, I planned on calling the police with an anonymous tip letting them know where to find Jay's body. The last thing I wanted them to find on him was a piece of paper with my name on it.

I tapped one of the cigarettes out of the pack and handed it to the woman. She took it with shaking fingers and put it to her lips.

I lit it with Jay's Zippo.

The woman closed her eyes and inhaled deep, then blew a thick cloud of smoke into the air above her. She looked down at the cigarette and rolled it between her fingers.

"You're taking me home?"

"Pella Valley."

She looked up at me, and I could tell she wanted to say something, but she didn't.

I asked her if she was okay.

She didn't answer—just took another drag off the cigarette and dropped it on the ground, letting it burn. Then she stood, slow, and walked past me toward the door.

18

The city lights faded behind us, leaving only trees and long, empty fields covered in white.

Neither of us spoke.

All I could think about was Anna. I tried to focus on seeing her again, and not on what was happening to her, or where she might be. I couldn't think about any of that until I had her back with me and I knew she was safe.

Then I'd think about all of it.

We were still several miles outside Pella Valley when the silence got to be too much. I could feel my thoughts spinning away from me, and I had to do something to refocus and settle my mind, so I started talking.

Once I got started, I couldn't stop.

At first, I asked her about her husband. I wanted to know all about him, and how he did what he did, but she didn't answer me, and I didn't press.

Instead, I tried to explain why I did what I did. I wanted her to know that this wasn't who I was, but I didn't know where to start. So I started at the beginning.

I told her about Beth.

I told her how we'd met, where we were married, and how we'd found out she was pregnant two days before I was deployed. I told her how I'd thought about Beth every day and night while I was gone.

Then I told her about Anna, how she was born while I was in Afghanistan, and how I'd missed the first two years of her life. I told her how my daughter didn't know me when I came home, but that it was okay because I barely knew myself.

The woman listened without saying a word, but it didn't matter. Talking helped keep my mind off Anna and what I'd brought into our lives. I didn't want a conversation. I wanted a confession.

Then I told her about the accident.

This time, she turned and looked at me as I spoke.

"I went in to identify her body, but there was never any doubt. They warned me about the injuries, but I had to see her." I hesitated. "When I left, they handed me a small envelope with her wedding ring inside and told me I should focus my energy on my daughter. So that's what I did."

The woman looked away.

"The frame of the car collapsed, and my daughter was pinned inside. The front part of her skull—" I stopped talking and ran my hand along my forehead, tracing the line of Anna's scar from memory. "The doctors told me she wouldn't read or speak again, but she proved them wrong."

The woman didn't say anything, and I stopped talking. We drove the rest of the way to Pella Valley in silence.

Several times I wanted to apologize for what we did to her, but each time I tried to form the words, they seemed too small, too meaningless.

It wasn't enough to be sorry, and by the time we pulled into Pella Valley and I saw the car wash at the far end of the main street, I'd given up on trying to explain why I did what I did.

There was no point.

Nothing I could say would make it right.

• • •

The car wash was a one-level brick building with two open bays and a single yellow light mounted in the center. There were two industrial vacuums at the corner, and a white picket fence surrounding a weatherworn silo that rose out of the shadows and towered over it all.

I pulled in and parked along the side of the building facing the entrance and shut off the engine. The night was quiet and dark and no cars passed along the street.

I looked at my watch.

I'd made it with five minutes to spare.

I turned to the woman and said, "We're early. He should be here any minute."

Silence.

I could feel the adrenaline buzzing through me, making it impossible to sit still. I tried my best, but it was no use. Eventually, I opened my door and got out.

The woman turned and watched me, silent.

I walked around to the back of the van and stood by the white picket fence and looked out over the long field stretching into darkness. I could hear a train somewhere in the distance. The sound, a soft and steady pulse, helped calm my nerves, and almost made it possible for me to think clearly.

Almost.

Something about being out here, so far removed from the city, bothered me. I went over all the reasons I could think of why he'd want to meet way out here, but none of them seemed to fit.

All I could do was wait and see.

At exactly ten o'clock, a wave of headlights passed over me. I turned and saw a black Town Car and a black SUV pull into the parking lot and stop side by side. Their headlights shone bright, making it impossible to see.

The wait was over.

• • •

I walked around and stood in front of the van. For a moment, no one moved, then all the doors opened at once, and I could see glimpses of shadows moving behind the headlights.

One of the shadows stepped forward, silhouetted by the headlights. He was alone, and he walked with a cane.

He stopped halfway.

I stood there, waiting for him to say something. When he didn't, I went around to the passenger side and opened the door and helped the woman out of the van.

She ran her hands over the wrinkles in her clothes, then straightened herself and started walking toward the man.

She'd gone a few feet when I said, "I'm sorry."

The woman stopped.

At first, I thought she'd keep walking, but instead, she turned and came back, stopping in front of me, her eyes never leaving mine.

I told her, "I wish I could take it all back."

The woman reached up, slow, and ran her fingertips over my cheek, soft and gentle. Then she pulled her hand away and slapped me, hard.

The sudden sting brought tears to my eyes. It didn't hurt as much as it shocked me. All I could do was stand there, staring, unable to speak.

The woman turned and walked away, fading into the lights. When she reached the old man, he wrapped his arms around her, pulling her close.

I stood there, watching for Anna and waiting.

The old man said something I didn't catch, then all at once there was movement behind the SUV's headlights. People were shouting, lights flashed red and blue, and two cop cars turned off the road into the parking lot.

"No."

I looked back, but there was nowhere to go.

Several men ran in from either side and up from the field behind me. They were screaming at me, telling me to get on the ground.

"No!"

I felt the first set of hands on my shoulder, and I reached up out of instinct and twisted the man's wrist at the joint. He cried out in pain, and I spun him away, running toward the old man.

"Where is my daughter?"

The old man saw me coming. He turned and stepped in front of his wife, shielding her. He didn't flinch, and he didn't back away. He just stood there, waiting.

I almost got to him, but before I did, several hands grabbed me and took me down. I fought, but there were too many of them. They swarmed over me, grabbing my arms, handcuffing me, pushing my face into the asphalt. I screamed at them as the old man climbed into the Town Car with his wife and drove away.

Once they were gone, someone said, "Hold him up."

Then I was up, on my knees.

My mind was blazing. Everything around me burned red and screamed black. My hands felt slick, and I realized, on some distant level, that the handcuffs had dug into my wrists, and I was bleeding.

I didn't care.

I kept screaming for them to stop him, that he had my daughter, but they didn't listen.

I fought harder, screamed until my throat ripped.

Eventually, a sheriff's deputy stepped forward with his baton cocked over his shoulder. I knew what was coming, but I didn't care.

I couldn't stop.

The deputy swung the baton, striking the bridge of my nose. I felt it go in a bright explosion of white.

After that, there was only darkness.

1 9

"Matt, wake up."

Beth's head is resting on my shoulder. She looks up at me and runs her hand down my bare chest then pokes my ribs. "Come on, you have to get up."

I reach for her hand and kiss it, feeling the soft warmth of her fingers against my lips. Then I roll over and face her, pulling the sheet up, covering us both.

I kiss her, breathe her in. "Not yet," I say.

"You have to."

I run my hand down her body, feeling her next to me, her skin alive against mine. "I want to stay with you."

"You can't."

I kiss her neck, work my way down.

Beth arches against me.

For a moment, I'm lost in her. Then I feel her hands on the sides of my head, lifting my face up to hers. She's staring at me, and her eyes are clear and warm and perfect, the color of autumn.

"Wake up, Matt."

"But—"

Beth puts a finger to my lips, stopping me. Then she bends forward, kissing me long and soft. When she pulls away, there are tears in her eyes.

"She's waiting for you."

I stare at her, not understanding.

Beth leans toward my ear, whispers, "Forever and always. Do you remember?"

I nod, feeling the tears press behind my eyes.

Beth smiles, kisses me once more.

"Then wake up."

• • •

I opened my eyes and inhaled sharp.

My clothes were soaked through, and cold water ran off my skin onto the floor. I tried to sit up, and the room spun around me.

There was a deputy standing in front of me holding a dripping plastic mop bucket. He watched me, birdlike, his shaved head tilted to the side.

"He lives."

There were two fluorescent bulbs in the ceiling buzzing a cold green light over the room. They were bright, and it took my eyes a minute to adjust. Once they did, I saw that I was in a large cement cell. There was a thick metal door open at one end, and two cement beds attached to the walls on either side. In the middle of the room was a metal toilet and sink. The floor was smooth and it slanted toward a drainage trench cut along the back wall.

The deputy with the bucket stepped back, and for the first time, I saw that we weren't alone.

There was another sheriff's deputy standing just inside the door. This one was younger, wide-eyed. He leaned against the wall, out of the way, shifting his weight from one foot to the other.

Standing next to him was a man in a charcoal-gray suit. He was tall, dark hair cut short, and he carried a black leather briefcase in his hand.

At first, I thought he might be my lawyer, but then he leaned forward to sit on the cement bed across from me, and I noticed the gun in the shoulder holster under his coat.

I saw another man kneeling in the far corner of the room. There was something familiar about him. He was older, and his thin white hair stood off his head in every direction. He had dirt on his clothes, and there was blood around his mouth and streaked down the front of his shirt.

His eyes were swollen shut, his face bruised.

He was holding a white rosary in both hands.

I stared at him for a long time, trying to remember where I'd seen him, but my thoughts were clouded, and it took a while before I remembered.

Then I did.

He was the driver. He'd been parked across the street from the salon that afternoon.

"I know you," I said. "You're—"

The older deputy stepped forward and punched me. The blow snapped my head back, and sent jagged shards of pain tearing through my brain. I reached up, holding my nose in both hands, and stayed like that until the pain began to fade. When I pulled my hands away, they were covered in blood.

I didn't say anything else.

A minute later, there were footsteps in the hall. I waited until they stopped, then I looked up.

The old man was standing in the doorway.

• • •

Seeing him brought it all back, and I could feel my muscles tense. I started to get up, but the deputy stepped in and pushed me back down, holding me there.

I looked up at the old man and said, "We had a deal. Where is she?"

He stared at me, didn't speak.

"Where is my daughter?"

The old man stayed in the doorway, watching me, hands folded over the top of his cane. Then he stepped in and crossed the room to where the driver was kneeling in the corner. He stood behind him, then reached down and put a hand on his shoulder.

The driver jumped at the man's touch and made a low cry in the base of his throat.

The old man patted his shoulder and made a slow shushing sound that came out like a hiss. He said something in Spanish that I didn't understand. When he finished, the driver looked up at him, his swollen eyes wide, and shook his head, talking fast through the tears.

The old man listened until the driver's voice broke off into sobs, then he held his hand out to him, palm down.

The driver took it and kissed it and pressed it against his face, repeating the same words over and over.

"*Lo siento, lo siento, perdoname por favor.*"

The two of them stayed like that for a long time, then the old man turned to the younger sheriff's deputy standing just inside the door.

The deputy looked around, frowned, and backed out of the room.

I listened to his footsteps trail off down the hall.

Once he was gone, the old man pulled his hand away and crouched down next to the driver. He whispered something to him, and the man nodded, wiping the tears from his cheeks.

The old man patted the driver on the back, then he stood and nodded to the man in the gray suit.

The man reached into his jacket and pulled out a small-caliber handgun. He took a suppressor tube from his pocket and attached it to the end of the gun barrel.

The driver didn't notice. He just stared down at the rosary, praying, wiping tears from his battered face.

I couldn't move.

I watched everything unfold in front of me. I wanted to scream out for them to stop, but I had no voice. At one point I tried to stand, but the man next to me closed his hand over my shoulder and held me in place. When I looked at him, he shook his head.

The driver never saw it coming.

The man in the gray suit came up behind him and held the gun against the base of his skull. He fired one shot with no hesitation, severing the man's spinal cord. His body jerked back then fell forward, hitting the wall. He stayed there for a moment, his muscles convulsing in short, violent hiccups, before his body slipped down to the floor.

I watched the blood pool under him then trail off and gather in the drainage trench along the wall.

I didn't say a word.

I'd seen men die before, more than once, but that had been war. I'd never seen anything like this, and I could feel something inside me shutting down. I told myself it wasn't happening, that I wasn't seeing what I knew I was seeing. I told myself it wasn't real, but of course it was.

I stared at the driver's body until the convulsions stopped and the older deputy let go of my shoulder and stepped away. The air in the room was hot and felt thick, making it hard to breathe. When I finally looked up, the old man was standing over me, watching me, his eyes empty and cold.

I laughed.

I couldn't help it.

It came from somewhere deep inside, and once I got started, I didn't think I'd ever be able stop.

Of course, I was wrong.

2 0

The man in the gray suit opened the briefcase and took out a wrinkled sheet of yellow legal paper. He smoothed it and handed it to the old man.

He looked at the paper then held it out to me.

I didn't take it.

"Is she safe?"

The old man ignored the question. "I want to know about the people on this list. Who are they?"

He offered the paper again, but I didn't need to look at it. I recognized the paper, and I knew where he got it.

"That's not mine."

"It was in your pocket."

"I took it from someone else."

"Who?"

I shook my head.

The old man sighed and took a pair of reading glasses from his pocket and slipped them on. He read down the list of names, one by one. When he finished, he stared at me over the top of his glasses and said, "You know these people?"

"No," I said. "I don't."

"Your name is on here."

I nodded.

"What is the plot against my family?"

"Plot?" I tried to say more, but I stumbled over my words. "I don't—"

"Who else was involved?"

"Involved?" I looked over the old man's shoulder at the man standing behind him. "There's no plot. It was just a job."

"A job."

"That's right." I could feel my mind spinning away from me, and I bit down hard on the insides of my cheeks, letting the pain pull me back. "Just tell me she's safe."

The old man turned to the deputy. "A chair, please."

The deputy went out.

For a while the room was silent except for the slow drip of blood running from the trench into the drain. When the deputy came back, he had a metal folding chair. He opened it and set it in front of me.

The old man eased down onto the chair and crossed one leg over his knee. He set the yellow paper on his lap and leaned back, staring at me, tapping his cane on the cement floor.

"Do you know who I am, Mr. Caine?"

"No," I said. "Not really."

The old man smiled. "You didn't think it wise to find out even the most basic details of the man whose wife you were planning on kidnapping?"

"It wasn't my plan," I said. "I was hired to drive."

The old man nodded. "Yet it was you who contacted me. It was you who demanded I pay a ransom for the safe return of my wife. And it was you alone who arrived to pick up the money." He paused. "That seems like a great deal of responsibility for a man just hired to drive."

I wanted to explain, but I knew it wouldn't make a difference, so I kept my mouth shut.

The old man stared at me for a moment longer, then he took a deep breath and said, "To be honest, there's not much you would've discovered. Other than occasional charity work, I've made it a priority of mine to keep a low profile over the years. I've found it makes things easier." He paused. "My name is Roman Pinnell. My wife, who you've already met, is called Rose."

I didn't say anything.

"Now, Mr. Caine, I'd like you to tell me who else was involved in this job of yours."

"No one," I said. "It was me and the guy who had that paper. That's it."

"I find that difficult to believe."

"It's the truth."

"And this other person, where is he now?"

I hesitated. "He's dead."

Pinnell's eye twitched, and I felt a streak of ice run all the way down my spine. I thought about expanding on my answer, but I decided it would be better to keep quiet.

For a long time, neither of us said a word. Finally, Pinnell sat forward and took off his reading glasses. He slipped them into the inside pocket of his coat then turned and nodded to the man in the gray suit.

The man reached for the briefcase on the bed across from me. He dialed the combination, popped the locks, and took out a small leather case.

Pinnell brushed his knee with the side of his hand. "My wife is flying home tomorrow."

I was staring at the leather case, and I barely heard him. When I snapped back, I wasn't sure what to say, so I didn't say anything. As it turned out, I didn't need to.

Pinnell kept talking.

"Even after all these years, she's never quite adapted to life in the city." He smiled. "Did you know, the village where we grew up has fewer than one hundred souls." He nodded, waved a hand in the air. "I will miss her, but I can hardly blame her for wanting to return home, especially in light of recent events."

"My daughter," I said. "She shouldn't suffer because of me."

"Everyone suffers for those they love," Pinnell said. "It can't be avoided."

"She's a child," I said. "She doesn't deserve—"

"Deserve?"

Pinnell laughed. The sound came out in one long, unbroken breath, hollow and humorless, like a dry wind.

I waited for him to say something else, but he didn't.

"She's innocent," I said. "She's a little girl. She doesn't know—"

"Mr. Caine."

I stopped talking and listened.

"My only concern is the plot against my family." He held up the yellow sheet of paper. "And with the names on this list."

"There is no plot," I said. "That's not my list. None of this has anything to do with me. I told you I was hired to drive."

"Who hired you?"

I motioned to the piece of paper. "The man who had that list. He was a friend."

"And now he's dead."

I nodded.

Pinnell leaned back, didn't speak.

"No one was ever going to hurt your wife," I said. "I wasn't going to let anything happen to—"

Pinnell lifted his cane and swung. The metal handle connected with the side of my head, and for an instant, everything went black. Then the pain hit, spreading down my spine and radiating out through my arms and legs. I couldn't breathe, and I couldn't speak.

The old man stood up, cane in hand. "You do not speak of my wife."

I looked up at him and saw thick veins pulsing under the weathered skin on his neck. I could feel a steady pulse of blood running down the side of my face, and I waited, bracing myself for another blow.

It never came.

Instead, Pinnell just stood there, staring at me.

After a while, he turned away and motioned to the man in the gray suit. The man stepped forward carrying the small leather case.

2 1

I tried to ask what they were going to do, but the pain in the side of my head had spread, and my jaw felt heavy and numb, making it hard to speak.

The man in the gray suit unzipped the leather case and took out a syringe and a small glass vial.

The old man paced behind the folding chair. His cane clicked hard on the cement floor, and the sound echoed through the cell.

I watched the man in the gray suit uncap the syringe and push the needle into the vial and pull the plunger. When the barrel was full, he held the syringe up to the light and tapped out the air bubbles.

I found my voice. "What are you going to do?"

Pinnell stopped pacing and turned to face me. "I've never been a patient man, Mr. Caine. It's always been a failing of mine, one of many I'm afraid, but one I'm always looking to improve on."

"I told you," I said. "I don't know those names."

Pinnell reached up and rubbed the spot between his eyebrows with one finger. "Do you know the Bent Tree Gardens on the west side?"

I shook my head.

"They're lovely." Pinnell looked up and stepped closer. "Every morning I go there. Sometimes to walk, other times to find a quiet spot where I can sit alone and think, but I never miss a day." He paused. "The routine calms me, and I believe the daily practice has helped me discover ways to be more patient, although sometimes, like right now, that patience is tested."

Everything inside me turned cold.

Pinnell crossed the room to the corner and slowly knelt next to the driver's body. "I'd known this man for nearly twenty years. He swore loyalty to my wife, to protect her from harm, but he was lazy and he was arrogant. He allowed your team to take her in the light of day." He glanced over at me. "An absurd plan that only succeeded because of his total incompetence."

"There was no team," I said. "I told you, it—"

"He failed me."

The old man looked down at the body then reached up and put the first two fingers of his right hand into his mouth, pulling them out wet. He mumbled something that sounded like a prayer then pressed both fingers into the bullet wound in the back of the driver's neck, forcing them in deep.

It took effort, and I heard a series of wet pops as he worked them in up to his knuckles.

I felt my stomach turn.

The old man, still praying, pulled his fingers out. They were coated dark with blood.

He turned to me.

I shook my head and started to stand, but then the deputy stepped in behind me and wrapped his arm around my neck and squeezed. I fought him at first, trying to pull his arm away, but each time I did, he only squeezed tighter.

My vision wavered and the strength ran out of my arms.

I watched the old man get closer until he was standing over me. His eyes were half-closed. He was still praying.

No, not praying.

He was chanting.

I tried one more time to break free, but my strength was gone, and there was nothing I could do.

The old man pressed his bloody fingers against my forehead, running them down then across. When he pulled them away, he leaned in close and whispered something to me in Spanish that I couldn't understand. Then he stepped back and held out his hand, palm up.

The man in the gray suit handed him the syringe.

"No!"

I saw what was about to happen, and once again I tried to break free. I managed to roll to the side, using all the strength I had left, but it was still no use.

The old man leaned forward, and when he spoke, I could feel his breath, sour and moist, against my skin.

"I've known some unpleasant men in my life, Mr. Caine. The worst kinds of men." He reached down and grabbed my left wrist and pulled my arm out straight. "While they've proven to be useful from time to time, their tastes run in directions I find unsettling." He looked up at me. "Your daughter will be quite a prize for these men."

I stopped fighting.

I didn't think I'd heard him right. I couldn't have heard him right. The words swam together in my head.

"You will answer my questions truthfully, or I will turn your daughter over to these men and their proclivities." He tapped the bend in my arm with his finger. "She is quite young. She will not understand what is happening to her, only that it is happening because of you." He paused. "I'll make sure of that."

The deputy behind me tightened his grip.

"She will expect you to help her, of course. What little girl wouldn't look for their father during such a terrifying time? But you will not be there for her. And when her suffering finally ends, she will be alone, knowing you never came."

I couldn't speak, but I managed to twist my head just enough to open my mouth and bite down hard on the deputy's wrist.

I tasted blood.

The deputy cried out, and his grip loosened.

For a second, I was able to breathe again. I sat up, reaching for the old man, but the deputy recovered quick and pulled me back, regaining his grip.

Pinnell was smiling.

"Incredible, isn't it?" His eyes were sharp and clear. "There is nothing more powerful than the desire to protect one's children when they are in danger. It is an utterly overwhelming emotion, and impossible to explain to someone who isn't a parent."

I tried to pull free. I wanted to tell him that I'd answer his questions, tell him whatever he wanted to know. But the deputy's grip was too tight, and there was no air.

My voice was barely a whisper.

Again, Pinnell grabbed my wrist and straightened my left arm. This time he pressed the needle into the vein just below the bend. There was a moment of icy cold that spread up my arm, across my chest, and into my brain.

Slowly, the deputy behind me let go.

I slumped forward.

"I'll tell you," I said. "Please."

There was low buzz building in the center of my head, branching out, turning all my muscles soft. I could barely keep my eyes open, but I didn't care.

It didn't matter anymore.

"Whatever you want to know," I said. "I'll tell you."

Pinnell reached out and gently touched my shoulder. "Yes," he said. "You certainly will."

PART III

2 2

The world came back in waves.

The older deputy was standing in the corner. He had a long green hose in his hand and was spraying the blood off the walls into the drainage trench along the floor. His left forearm was wrapped in a clean white bandage, and he had his back to me.

He was whistling "Wild Blue Yonder."

I watched him, but my eyes kept drifting to the hose. Following it from his hand, across the floor in front of me, and out the open cell door into the hallway.

I stared at it for a long time.

Something about the open door was important, but I couldn't understand why. My thoughts were thick, and whatever I was searching for fell just out of reach.

I tried to sit up. When I did, the walls wavered in and out, and I felt my stomach lurch.

I rolled to the side just in time.

The deputy turned and yelled, "Hey, Goddamn it!"

I saw him point the hose, and then I was wet.

The water soaked my hair and ran over my skin, dripping onto the floor under me.

"You think I want to clean this shit?"

I tried to breathe.

Once again I felt my stomach clench, but this time nothing came up. When the feeling passed, I rolled onto my back and folded my arms over my eyes.

I could feel the water soaking into my clothes and pooling under me, but I didn't care. My breathing was thin, and the shadows seemed to swirl around me like tiny fingers, reaching in and dragging me down, pulling me back into darkness.

• • •

"Wake up."

The voice was faraway, insistent.

I felt a sharp, stinging pain against my face, then hands on my shirt, lifting me up.

Again the voice.

"You have to get up. Now."

I opened my eyes and the bright fluorescent light burned through me. The younger deputy was standing in front of me, slapping my face. When he saw that my eyes were open, he stopped and stepped back.

"Come on," he said. "We don't have much time."

I watched him for a second then leaned forward, elbows on knees, and held my head in my hands. The pain behind my eyes was worse. I tried to remember what had happened, but all that came were flashes of faces and voices, all of them hidden behind a haze of images and dreams.

The air in the cell was wet and cold, and I saw water dripping down the walls and running pink toward the trench.

I stared at it and thought of nothing at all.

"Hey."

I looked up at the deputy, tried to focus. His skin was smooth and unlined, and I noticed a ring of tiny blackheads along the side of his nose.

"How old are you?" I asked.

He ignored me, said, "If you want see your daughter again, you need to come with me right now."

The words brought me back, not all the way, but far enough to remind me of where I was and what was happening. I could feel some of the strength returning to my legs, and I stretched them out in front of me and tried to stand.

The deputy offered his hand and helped me to my feet. The door to the cell was open at the far end of the room, and I stared at it, trying to piece everything together. I knew where I was, but the details were faded, lost in the mist.

Then it all started to come back.

This time, the waves came faster, each one unfolding a small slip of memory: Pinnell, the man in the charcoal-gray suit, the driver.

Oh, God, the driver.

I tried to focus, but my thoughts were scattered, and each time I put something together, another part would drift away into the slow white nothing.

Then I remembered Anna, and everything changed.

"Can you walk?"

I looked at the deputy and nodded.

"Good," he said. "Because we don't have much time."

I thought about the older deputy and said, "Where did they—"

"They took him somewhere." The deputy pointed to the corner where the driver's body had been. "I don't know where, and I don't care. I don't want any part of it." He shook his head. "I don't mind looking the other way for a few extra bucks now and then, but I didn't sign up for murder, or for whatever happened to your kid."

"What do you know?"

"I know if you don't get the hell out of here, you're next. These guys don't fuck around, and I won't be able to help you again."

I glanced over at the open door. "You want me to just walk out of here?"

"My keys are on the desk," he said. "My cruiser is parked out front. Take it and go."

"What about you?" I asked. "They'll know—"

"They won't know shit." He reached down and unclipped the Taser on his belt and handed it to me. "Use this."

"What?"

"You snuck up on me when I thought you were out cold. You grabbed it and that's all I remember." He waved his hand toward the door. "I've only been here for two months, and they already think I'm a rookie fuckup. They'll believe it."

I looked down at the Taser in my hand.

"They're coming back," he said. "If you don't go now, you won't get another chance." He pointed to the cell door. "Lock me in when you leave. That'll buy you some time."

I nodded.

The deputy stepped closer, pointed at the Taser.

He didn't have to tell me again.

• • •

I did what he asked and closed the cell door behind me, locking him inside. The hallway was bright, and I reached out, bracing myself against the wall as I made my way toward the front of the building.

I came around the corner and through a heavy door that opened into the front office. There were three desks in two rows behind the counter, along with a copier, a water cooler, and several filing cabinets covered with the kinds of plants that are hard to kill.

I looked down at the desks, but I didn't see keys on any of them. I felt the panic hit hard, then I saw a silver key ring on the desk beside the counter. I picked it up and walked around the front and through the main doors.

I stopped on the steps leading down to the parking lot and looked at the snow-covered trees and the antique street-lights lining the road. The air was cold, and I breathed it in, letting it clear my head.

It helped a little, but not much.

Above me the sky was dark and filled with snow. The thin flakes swirled in the air like untethered stars. It was beautiful, and it was hard to look away.

On the road, a car passed, snapping me back.

I looked down at the deputy's keys in my hand, then up at the parking lot and the three cruisers parked alongside the building. Each car had a number, and I matched it with the number stamped on one of the keys.

It worked.

I slid the key into the ignition, and the engine started on the first try. I rolled the windows down then put the car in gear and backed out of the parking lot.

By the time I turned onto the highway, heading north toward the city, the cold night air had done its job.

I almost felt alive again.

2 3

Traffic on the highway was light, and the city skyline glowed in the distance, reflecting bright under a low overhang of clouds. I kept the radio off and the windows down as I drove, and I forced myself to focus on one thing.

Finding Roman Pinnell.

I didn't think about Anna. I wouldn't let myself. I knew if I did, if I let my guard down even for a second, emotion would take over and I'd make mistakes. And if I made mistakes, I'd lose her forever.

I was not going to let that happen.

As I drove, I tried to figure out a plan. My thoughts were still heavy and slow, but I had a good idea of where I needed to start.

When I got to my exit, I pulled off the highway and drove through my neighborhood to my house. There was no one on the street, but I pulled around back to the alley just to be safe.

I stopped behind my house and watched the windows for any signs of life. When I was sure it was clear, I shut off the engine and stepped out and walked along the back fence to the gate. I reached over and popped the latch.

The hinges were rusted and loud.

I looked around to see if anyone heard, but nothing had changed. There was only wind and shadow and snow.

I crossed through the yard to my back door.

It was locked.

They'd taken my keys after they'd picked me up, so my options were limited. I tried a couple of windows, but I knew the result would be the same.

That left only one way inside.

I took off my shirt and held it over one of the small window squares on the back door then hit it hard with my elbow. The glass popped out, shattering on the floor.

I reached through and unlocked the door.

The house was warm and silent. I stood in the kitchen and let my eyes adjust to the darkness. Then I walked out to the living room and down the hall toward my bedroom. When I got there, I threw my bloody shirt in the corner and hit the light switch.

Nothing happened, and I remembered the power was out.

I crossed to the nightstand next to the bed, opened the top drawer, and grabbed a red LED flashlight. I pushed the button and the light came on bright.

I turned and opened the closet.

My clothes were hung on the rack, and there were several boxes stacked on the floor and on the top shelf. I grabbed a new shirt then put the flashlight in my mouth and reached up and pushed a few boxes aside until I felt the handle of my gun case.

I pulled it out and set the case on the bed and dialed in the combination. The latches popped, and I opened the lid.

My .45 was inside, along with two loaded clips and a full box of ammo.

I slid one of the clips into the gun, loaded a round, and checked the safety. Then I pocketed the other clip and the extra ammo and walked down the hall to the bathroom.

I put the .45 in my belt and set the flashlight on the sink, pointing up, then leaned forward and examined my face in the mirror. It didn't look as bad as I'd expected. Most of the blood was gone—probably washed off from the hose in the cell—but there was a deep gash along the right side where the old man's cane had hit, and another over the bridge of my nose.

Not too bad, considering.

I turned on the water and started washing the remaining blood from my face and chest. I'd gotten most of it off when I heard a noise coming from the front of the house.

I shut off the water and listened.

There were footsteps on the porch.

I took the gun from my belt, switched off the flashlight, and walked out of the bathroom and stood in the doorway between the hall and the living room.

I heard the thin chime of keys. Then the lock turned.

I lifted the gun, clicked the safety, and took aim.

The door opened to moonlight, and a dark silhouette stepped into the house. I sighted the gun as the figure turned and closed the door.

For a moment, nothing moved.

I could hear my heartbeat, loud in the center of my head, and I blinked hard, trying to push away whatever fog was left.

I held my breath.

There was a small click, then a beam of light came on and scanned the room. When it passed over me, the figure jumped and dropped the flashlight.

My finger twitched on the trigger.

I pulled back at the last second.

I turned on my flashlight and shone it on Carrie. She was standing in the doorway, her hands over her mouth, her eyes wide. She stared at me for a moment then dropped her hands to her chest and said, "Matt?"

"What are you doing here?"

"I saw the light," she said. "I thought it might be you. I wanted to see if—" She stopped, looked around. "You didn't find her?"

"Not exactly."

"What does that mean?"

I slid the gun into my belt and turned back to the bathroom. "It means I don't have her yet."

"Where is she?"

I didn't answer. Instead, I set the flashlight back on the sink and finished scrubbing the blood off my skin.

Carrie followed me, stopping in the doorway.

When I looked up at her in the mirror, she gasped.

"Oh my God." She stepped into the bathroom and pulled at my shoulder. "Let me look."

I told her it was fine.

She reached up and felt the sides of my nose with her fingertips. "You need a doctor."

"No, I don't."

Carrie put her hands on either side of my head and ran her thumbs over my cheeks and around my eyes. "Does anything else hurt? Is anything else broken?"

I reached up and grabbed her wrists. "I'm fine, Carrie."

For a moment, neither of us moved. Then Carrie's eyes filled with tears. She leaned forward and rested her head against my chest. I put my arms around her, and we stood like that for a long time.

After a while, I said, "I need you to do something."

"What?"

"I want you to leave town for a few days. Get as far away as you can."

Carrie frowned. "I'm not going anywhere."

"You can't be involved in this," I said. "I don't want you to get hurt because of me."

Carrie pulled away. "You're serious?"

"Just until this is settled."

There was a look in Carrie's eyes I'd never seen before, and I didn't like it. I tried to explain why I wanted her to leave, but before I could, she pulled her arm away and slapped me hard across the face.

I stopped talking.

The look in Carrie's eyes didn't change, and neither of us moved. Then she slapped me again. This time the blow rattled my broken nose and sent sparks of light spiraling behind my eyes.

I lifted my hand and said, "Enough."

"You don't think I'm involved?"

At first I thought she was going to hit me again, and I braced myself for the blow. But she didn't. Instead, she stepped back and ran her fingers under her eyes, wiping away tears, then turned and walked down the hall toward Anna's room.

I stayed where I was, listening to the silence of the house and trying to decide if I should go after her. Part of me wanted to reach out for her, grab her, and hold her until everything went away, but I knew better.

Nothing I could do would take this away.

Not for either of us.

2 4

I waited a few minutes before walking down the hall to Anna's room. Her door was half-open, and in the shadows, I could see that all the drawings and signs had been taken down. I stopped outside and stared at the thin split in the wood where the tip of the knife had gone through, then I reached out and pushed the door open.

Carrie was sitting on Anna's bed, crying, staring down at her hands folded in her lap.

Anna's room was spotless. The bloodstained carpet by her door had been cut out in a large square, revealing the scarred hardwood floor beneath.

"Did you do this?" I asked.

"I had to do something," Carrie said. "I couldn't stand knowing it was there."

I stepped into the room and checked the other side of the door. The wood had been scrubbed clean, but the deep gash where the knife went in was wide and visible.

"I'm sorry I hit you."

"No," I said. "I understand."

"I don't think you do." She looked up at me, her eyes wet and bright. "I was here when they took her. I couldn't do anything."

"No one is blaming you," I said. "It's okay."

"It's not okay!" Carrie's breath caught in her throat and she looked away. "It's not okay."

"You did everything you could."

Carrie laughed to herself.

"Come on," I said. "Don't do that."

"I listened to her scream when they dragged her out of her room. That was all I could do."

I opened my mouth to speak, but she stopped me.

"I saw what happened. I was here." She paused, stared at me. "Don't ever tell me I'm not involved."

My legs felt weak, and I sat beside her on the bed. For a while, neither of us said anything. Then Carrie moved closer and leaned her head against my shoulder.

I put my hand on her leg.

"What are we going to do?" she asked.

"We're going to get her back."

Carrie looked up at me. "What happened, Matt? Who were those people? What did they do with her?"

I thought about it, but I couldn't find the words. "I don't know where to start."

Carrie reached up and touched my chin, turning my face to hers. Then she leaned in and pressed her lips against mine.

I didn't stop her, and I didn't pull away.

I let myself drift in her.

When we broke, she slid her fingers down my cheek and said, "Start at the beginning."

So I did.

• • •

I told Carrie everything, starting with the night I met Jay in the bar. By the time I got to the old woman and the warehouse down by the river, Carrie was up, pacing the room. When I told her what happened in the holding cell in Pella Valley, she waved a hand in front of her face and said, "I don't want to hear any more."

"There's not much more to tell," I said. "That's when I came here."

"For your gun?"

"That's right."

"What exactly were you going to do with it?"

I thought about my answer, then said, "I'm going to find Roach and get Pinnell's address."

"And then?"

"And then I'm going to find him and make him tell me where she is." I paused and looked up at Carrie. "And if he doesn't tell me, I'm going to kill him."

"My God, Matt!"

"Do you have a better idea?"

"Yes." Carrie sat next to me, took my hands. "Let's go to the police. They have special departments that handle this kind of thing. They can help us."

"If I go to the police, he's going to kill her."

"He won't find out," she said. "I can go myself. I can talk to them and tell them the situation. They can track her down a lot faster than you can."

"No, they can't."

"Matt, please."

"Listen to me," I said. "We can't go to the police, not now, not ever, do you understand?"

"But—"

"If I do this right, if I can get to him, I can bring her home."

"He'll kill you."

"Maybe," I said. "But if I go to the police, Anna is as good as dead. I don't know who this guy is, but he knows things. He has the sheriff's department in Pella Valley working for him. God knows who else."

"That's crazy, Matt. No one—"

"You saw what he did here," I said. "I told you what happened to me. It's too much of a risk."

"Then I'm coming with you."

I shook my head, slow.

"Don't you dare," she said. "You can't go off and expect me to sit here and wait for you like I'm—"

"I need you to stay out of it, please."

"I can't sit here helpless, Matt. I won't."

I got up and took a marker and a piece of yellow construction paper from Anna's desk. "I'm going to try and call you tonight, but if you don't hear from me by morning, there's someone—"

"Don't hear from you?"

"—I need you to call."

"Matt, don't do this." Carrie got up and stood next to me. She put her hand on my shoulder and pulled me around to face her. "Don't go running after this guy, please. You're going to get yourself killed."

I told her I'd be fine, but my voice sounded weak and unsure, even to me.

"Matt?"

I turned back to the yellow construction paper and finished writing out the address. "There's an old friend of mine I want you to go see. His name is Brian Murphy. He owns a bar over in—"

"No." She stepped back, shaking her head. "Not him."

"I want you to talk to him," I said. "If anyone gives you a hard time, tell them you're there to see Murphy, and that you have a message for him from me. He'll talk to you."

"Please don't do this."

I handed her the paper with his address. "Tell him the situation and that you haven't heard from me."

"Oh, God."

"I want you to tell him to find Anna."

"What?"

"If he says no, you tell him he owes me."

Carrie started to say something else, but she stopped herself and looked down at the paper. I could see her hands shaking as she reached up and wiped away tears.

I held her shoulders and pulled her close.

"This is a last resort," I said. "I'm bringing her home. I don't care what I have to do."

Carrie stepped back and held up the paper. "Do you trust him?"

"With this? Yes."

"What makes you think he's going to risk his life and go after her? I mean, what's to stop him from ignoring this completely?"

I thought about it then said, "Nothing."

Carrie was quiet for a long time. "I hate feeling so helpless."

I reached out and lifted her chin until our eyes met, then I leaned in and kissed her. I wanted that kiss to say all the things I couldn't. I wanted it to tell her how sorry I was, and that no matter what happened, she wasn't to blame. But most of all, I wanted the kiss to take away all the pain I'd caused.

Of course, it didn't.

And when I pulled away, all I could taste was the salt of her tears on my lips.

2 5

I didn't like driving the police cruiser, so I took back roads all the way to Roach's place. When I got there, I parked down the street and walked the rest of the way to her building.

I buzzed her apartment.

There was no answer, and I tried again.

Still nothing.

I stepped back and looked around at the cars lining the block. There were two men sitting on a low flight of steps across the street, laughing and passing a bottle between them. I thought about asking them if they knew Roach and if they'd seen her, but decided against it.

The fewer people who saw me, the better.

I walked around the side of the building and looked up at Roach's apartment on the fourth floor. The windows were dark, and all at once the hopelessness of the situation hit me, and my stomach fell away.

I thought about what Carrie had said and wondered if she was right. I didn't see how I was going to find Anna on my own. She could be anywhere, and I had nothing to go on.

If I called the police and told them what I knew, there was a chance they could help.

No.

For the first time, I let myself think about Anna and where she might be and what might be happening to her.

It was all I needed.

I walked into the alley and stood under the fire escape. The ladder was pulled up, so I pushed one of the Dumpsters under it and climbed on top.

I jumped and grabbed the bottom rung and pulled myself onto the fire escape. It took a lot of my strength, and once I was up, I sat and leaned back against the building. My head felt light, and the constant dull pain behind my eyes turned sharp.

I ignored it and climbed the rusted metal stairs to the fourth floor and looked in Roach's window, shielding the light from the street with my hands.

The apartment was dark and empty.

I could see the coffee table Jay and I had sat around earlier that day while we went over his plan. For a second I was struck by how long ago that seemed, and how much had changed in such a short time.

I reached down and tried to open the window. It was locked, but the latch inside rattled loose and it didn't take much force to snap it open and push the window up.

I took the gun from my belt and ducked inside.

The air inside Roach's apartment was stale and smelled like old ashtrays and cooked meat. There was a McDonald's bag on the coffee table next to several crumpled napkins and a half-empty bottle of Smirnoff vodka.

Someone had been there since that afternoon.

I clicked the safety off on the .45 and walked through the living room toward the kitchen and looked in. There were dirty dishes stacked in the sink, and a garbage bag filled with tin cans next to the refrigerator. On the counter, two more empty vodka bottles.

I lowered the gun.

Roach had been here, and that meant she'd be back. I didn't like the idea of waiting for her, but I didn't see any other option. She handled the appointment books at the salon, and she knew where the old man lived. I wasn't going anywhere until she told me.

Outside in the hallway, someone laughed.

There was a thin sliver of light leaking in from under the door, and I crossed the room and looked out through the peephole. I saw a man and woman standing in front of the apartment across the hall. She had her arms around his neck as he held her hips, pinning her against the wall.

Eventually, she pushed him away and searched through a set of keys. He came up behind her and kissed her neck. She smiled, slid the key into the lock, and they both disappeared inside.

I watched their door close then stepped back.

I thought about my next move.

It occurred to me that Jay had been staying here. That meant some of his things had to be here. I didn't think I'd find anything important, but it was worth a shot.

I took one last look out the peephole then turned away from the door. I made it three steps before I stopped and looked back.

The chain on the front door was locked.

I stood there, staring at the rusted metal chain, letting the pieces fall together in my head.

The lock could only be fastened from the inside.

All at once, the gun felt heavy in my hand.

I turned and saw something move out of the corner of my eye. I lifted the gun, but I was too late.

The figure came in fast.

I had just enough time to register a baseball bat before I dropped down and covered my head with both hands.

The bat hit the wall just above my head, and tiny bits of plaster fell around me. I moved in, grabbing his arms and sweeping his legs out from under him.

We hit the floor hard.

I climbed on top, pinning his arms under my legs, and pulled my fist back, ready.

"Matt!"

A woman's voice.

"Roach?"

"Get the fuck off me."

I moved away, and Roach tried to sit up.

"What the fuck, Matt?"

"You could've killed me," I said.

"You broke into my apartment, asshole." Roach got to her feet and looked around for the bat. She found it, picked it up, and carried it out to the living room, mumbling to herself along the way.

I brushed the plaster dust from my clothes and hair.

My hands were shaking.

Roach grabbed the half-empty bottle of vodka from the coffee table and dropped onto the couch. "You're still alive, I see."

"Are you surprised?"

"Of course not," she said. "You've always been lucky." She paused, took a drink, and pointed at my face. "Or maybe not. What the hell happened to you?"

"It's nothing."

She nodded, quiet, then said, "What did you do with Jay's body?"

"Still at the warehouse."

She looked at me, and in the light coming through from the street, I saw that her eyes were red and swollen. Most of that, I figured, was from the vodka, but not all of it.

She'd been crying for a while.

"You left him there?"

I pushed myself up. "If it wasn't for you, he wouldn't be there to begin with."

Roach's eyes narrowed. "If you really believe that, then you didn't know him at all."

She had a point.

Jay went out exactly how everyone who ever knew him expected him to go out. It wasn't Roach's fault any more than the guy who sold him the shot that killed him.

Jay was dead because of Jay.

For a while, neither of us said anything. Roach took another drink and offered me the bottle.

"No." I slipped the gun back into my belt and said, "I need to talk to you."

"About?"

"An address," I said. "Her address."

Roach frowned. "Her who? I don't—" She stopped, and the realization showed on her face. "You're kidding."

I told her I wasn't.

Roach laughed, took another drink from the bottle, and said nothing.

2 6

"Can you get it?"

Roach stared at me. "Why?"

I didn't want to tell her about Anna, but I needed her help, and I didn't see any other way.

The news didn't seem to faze her. "So you want me to give you their home address?"

"And tell me what you can about her and her husband."

Roach laughed. "Here's what I know." She held up two fingers. "She's rich, and she gets her hair done twice a month. Any of that help?"

"Then just their address."

"I don't see what good it'll do," Roach said. "If they've got your kid, they're not going to take her home with them. They'll just dump her somewhere."

The words stung, but I kept going, trying to stay calm. "I don't know where they took her, but Pinnell knows, and he's going to tell me."

"Do you plan on just ringing the bell and asking him where he took her?"

"It's a start."

"It's fucking stupid, Matt."

I felt the anger glow inside me, but I managed to keep it in check. I reminded myself that Roach was hard to deal with at the best of times, and these were far from the best of times.

"What would you do?"

"I'm not the person to ask." She waved me off and leaned back on the couch. "I'll get you her address, but it'll have to wait until tomorrow. All that stuff is in the computer at work."

"Tomorrow?"

"If I can get in tomorrow."

I waited for her to explain. When she didn't, I asked, "Is there a problem?"

Roach motioned to the window with the bottle. "I was followed tonight. They were sitting outside when I got home."

"The two across the street on the steps?" I asked. "They're not following you."

"How do you know?"

"They're drunks," I said. "And you're paranoid."

"Fuck you, Matt."

"You're jumping at shadows," I said. "There's no one waiting for you out there."

"Check."

"I'm telling you."

"Check." She pointed the bottle at the window. "I'm not leaving if they're still there. It's up to you."

I stared at her, silent.

Roach frowned. "Well?"

I got up and walked to the front window and looked down over the street.

"Are they there?"

I didn't answer.

"Matt?"

The street outside was still and white with snow. The men I'd seen on the steps were gone, but there was someone else there now, standing under one of the lights across the street.

"Are they there?"

I told her they weren't.

"Then what is it?"

I didn't answer. Instead, I went around to the fire escape and opened the window. I stuck my head out and looked down. There was another man standing in the alley, smoking a cigarette.

"Shit."

Roach sat up. "They're out there, aren't they?"

"Someone's out there," I said. "Whoever they are, they weren't outside when I got here. It looks like they're waiting for us."

Roach pushed herself off the couch and grabbed the baseball bat. "Are they coming up here?"

"I don't think so."

Roach held the bat against her chest and paced the room. I went back to the front window and looked out at the street and cursed myself under my breath for being so careless. Coming here had been a mistake.

I should've known better.

If they didn't already know I'd made it out of the cell in Pella Valley, they sure as hell knew now.

"We need to go," I said. "Is there another way out of the building?"

"There's a back door, but we'll have to go down to the basement and through the laundry room."

"That'll have to do," I said. "Come on."

"And go where?" Roach held up her hand. "Where do you think we're going to go?"

I grabbed her silver coat off the arm of the couch and tossed it to her. "Anywhere but here."

Roach stared at me for a second then slipped her coat on and followed me to the door. When we got close, I held up my arm, stopping her.

"What?"

I pointed to the strip of light coming in from under the door. A shadow passed outside in the hall.

We stood, silent, waiting.

A second later, I heard the muffled clink of glass breaking. Then the hall light went out.

Someone was standing outside the door.

I took my .45 from my belt and nodded toward the window and the fire escape. "Outside. Go."

Roach didn't move, so I took her arm and pulled her along.

"Get your fucking hands off me."

I stopped, whispered, "Stay here if you want, but I'm leaving."

I opened the window to the fire escape and sat on the windowsill and zipped my coat. Then I slid the .45 into my belt and started to climb out.

Roach stood behind me, watching. "You said someone was down there. They'll see you."

I leaned out and checked again. Roach was right. The man was still there, standing in the alley. He would see me before I had a chance to get close.

I looked up.

When I pulled my head back in, I smiled.

Roach shook her head. "Not a chance."

"You got a better idea?"

"Yeah, we stay here and fight." She lifted the bat and motioned to me. "You've got a gun. We'll wait until he comes in and you shoot him."

"I'm not shooting anyone unless I have to."

"Well, aren't you fucking noble?"

I swung my leg out the window and looked back at her. "You coming or not?"

"To the roof?"

"It's the only way we get out of here."

"There's no way down once you're up there. We'll be stuck."

Behind her, the lock on the front door rattled.

"We don't have time for this."

Roach shook her head. "I'm staying here."

I tried to argue, but Roach stepped closer and pushed me onto the fire escape. "Go."

She shut the window and turned away.

Below, the man in the alley was pacing back and forth, leaving heavy tracks in the snow. I pressed against the wall and steadied myself. When I was ready, I reached for the ladder and started up.

I'd made it almost all the way to the top floor when I heard a loud crash from inside Roach's apartment. Roach yelled, then there was the unmistakable sound of a gunshot.

Then two more.

After that, silence.

27

The fire escape ended several feet below the roof. There was a dark window leading back inside, and a cement ledge lined with several stone gargoyles above me. The ledge ran along the length of the building, and I thought if I climbed onto the railing and jumped, I might be able to reach the ledge and pull myself up onto the roof.

It wasn't the best option, but it seemed like the only one I had left.

I steadied myself against the wall and put my foot on the top of the railing. Then I eased up, testing my weight before each move.

I heard voices below me and looked down. When I did, the world seemed to pinwheel around me, and the strength dropped out of my legs. I had just enough time to see a figure leaning out of Roach's window two floors below, then my foot slipped and I fell.

I landed hard on the railing, knocking the air out of my lungs. I teetered there, feeling my weight pull me over the edge. At the last second, I kicked out, desperately trying to arch back onto the platform. I managed to catch the railing with my foot and stop myself from falling all the way down to the alley below.

I pulled myself back onto the platform and slipped down to sitting. My heart was beating so hard in my chest that I could feel it in my throat. When I was ready, I pushed myself up and tried to catch my breath.

I glanced down at Roach's apartment and saw a man climbing out of her window and onto the fire escape. He was moving fast, and he had a gun in his hand.

I had to get up.

I wasn't about to try the ledge again, so that left one option. I stood and kicked the window, shattering the glass, then bent down and crawled through into a dark room filled with cardboard moving boxes.

At first, I thought I'd come in through a storage room, but that changed when the woman sitting on the couch in the corner started screaming.

I held up my hands and said, "I'm sorry."

It didn't help.

The woman kept screaming.

I got to my feet and wove my way past the boxes to the front door. I pulled it open, but it caught on the chain lock. I slammed it shut, slid the chain, and tried again. This time, the door opened easily, and I ran out into the hallway.

Behind me, the woman stopped screaming, but only for a minute. By the time I reached the utility door leading to the stairwell, she'd started again, and I knew the man on the fire escape had just come inside.

I waited for gunshots, but this time they never came.

I took my .45 from my belt and eased the utility door open. The stairwell was empty. I took one last look back then ran down the steps, taking them two at a time.

I'd made it down two floors when I heard the utility door open above me. Then a man's voice echoed through the stairwell.

"You can't get out," he said. "There's no place to go."

I kept running.

When I got to the second floor, I looked over the railing and saw two men coming up the stairs.

Above me, the man with the gun was coming down fast.

I pushed through the door onto the second floor and ran down the hallway. I checked a couple doors, all locked. Then I turned the corner and saw a kid, earbuds in his ears, step out from one of the apartments and into the hallway. He didn't notice me.

I came up behind him, gun drawn.

When he saw me, he pressed himself flat against the wall and said, "I don't have any money, man."

I motioned to the door and said, "Open it."

"There's nothing in there, I swear."

I could hear the men coming onto the second floor shouting, their footsteps heavy on the thin carpet.

I pointed the gun in the kid's face.

"Open the fucking door."

The kid reached down and unlocked the door and swung it wide.

I motioned back over my shoulder toward the growing sound of footsteps and said, "You should hide."

"What?"

I ran inside and locked the door behind me. The apartment was the same layout as Roach's place, only reversed. Instead of looking out over the alley, the window leading to the fire escape faced the empty street.

I pushed the window open and crawled out. I could hear voices from the hall, then the kid said, "He's in there."

I pulled the latch to lower the ladder, and the metal screeched. It dropped halfway to the street then stopped.

"Shit."

I kicked the side, but it wouldn't move.

I heard keys turning in the lock and the men moving outside the door. I looked over the edge of the fire escape at the sidewalk below. It was at least twenty feet down, and there was nothing to break my fall.

No choice.

I put my foot on the ladder and started down. When I got to the end, I let my feet hang out into nothing and climbed, hand over hand, down to the last rung and stayed there, still a good fifteen feet from the ground.

Above me, one of the men said, "He's down here."

I looked up and saw them climbing through the window and onto the fire escape.

I let go of the ladder and fell.

When I hit the ground, my leg slipped on the snow, and I felt something in my left knee pop.

The pain was incredible.

I tried to block it, tried to get to my feet, but each time I put weight on the leg, it folded under me.

There were footsteps on the metal fire escape above me, and I looked up. The two men were standing at the top of the ladder, staring down at me. One said something, then they turned and disappeared back into the apartment.

I pushed myself up, putting most of my weight on my right leg. The cruiser was parked at the end of the block, where I'd left it, and I started hobbling down the street toward it.

Each step sent a sharp, stabbing pain up my leg and into my spine, but I didn't stop moving. There wasn't much time, and it wouldn't take long for the two men to get down the stairs. Once they did, they'd come for me, and I was in no condition to run.

I was almost to the cruiser when I heard footsteps. I turned and saw the third man coming up behind me. He was holding a silver handgun with a black suppressor.

I took the .45 from my belt and fired as the other two came around the corner.

The sound echoed loud off the buildings around us, and the man dropped. I fired two more shots at the other two behind him, but the bullets went low, sparking against the sidewalk.

The men scattered.

It didn't give me much time, but it was enough.

I fired several more shots as I limped the rest of the way to the cruiser. Each step felt like an electric shock, each one worse than the one before.

I climbed into the cruiser, expecting to hear shots tearing into the car, but they never came.

I started the engine and pulled away, and I didn't look back.

2 8

I drove fast.

I could feel the adrenaline pulsing through me, and every part of me seemed to shake. The pain in my knee had gotten worse, and whenever I moved my leg, my mouth would turn sour and my stomach would twist. Twice, I had to pull over and lean out of the car, and both times nothing came up but stomach acid.

After the second time, I leaned my head against the steering wheel and listened to the wind outside. My thoughts were spinning out of control, and nothing I did helped.

They'd known about Roach. They'd been waiting.

I felt like a fool for not expecting it. If Pinnell could find out about me, he would've had no problem tracing everything back to the salon.

Now, Roach was dead, and time was running out.

I was sure the news I'd made it out of Pella Valley had made its way back to the old man. That meant things were about to get more complicated. I still had to find Pinnell, but without Roach I didn't know where to begin.

Then it came to me.

I didn't like the answer, but I also knew I couldn't do this one alone.

Outside, a blue Jeep sped by. The radio was loud, and the heavy bass rattled the windows of the cruiser. I watched it disappear around the end of the block, then I reached out and put the car in gear.

My hand was no longer shaking.

I took it as a good sign.

• • •

Murphy's bar was a long, one-level brick building in the warehouse district. The door was metal, faded green, and there were two large front windows and a row of smaller, square windows along the sides. It was an easy place to miss if you didn't know what you were looking for.

There was a parking garage next door, and I pulled in and took a space as close to the front as I could. I didn't trust my knee to take me very far, but I wasn't about to park a stolen police cruiser in front of Murphy's place.

I was desperate, not stupid.

I shut off the engine and opened the door. When I slid my leg out, my knee screamed at me, and tiny beads of sweat formed on my skin.

I closed my eyes and waited for the pain to pass. Once it did, I tried again, easing my legs out and pushing myself up to standing. When I felt steady, I put a hand against the wall and moved slowly through the parking garage and out onto the street.

By the time I got to Murphy's, my knee had started to loosen up a little. I stood outside and tried to collect myself. Then I pushed the door open and walked in.

There was no one inside except for a woman standing behind the bar holding a clipboard. She was young and had pomegranate-red hair that fell around her face in tight curls. When she saw me, she set the clipboard down and watched me ease over and sit on one of the barstools.

She came over slow.

I leaned out and grabbed a chair from one of the tables and pulled it close. I set my leg on top of it and tried my best to ignore the pain.

The woman stood behind the bar, watching me.

"Can I get a bag of ice?" I asked.

"What else?"

"That's it."

The woman frowned. "This isn't a hospital, buddy. Order a drink or hobble your busted ass out of here."

I stared at her, smiling despite the pain, and said, "Jameson's, neat."

She stared at me for a moment longer, her eyes narrow, then turned back to the bar and grabbed the Jameson bottle from the shelf. She poured the drink and set it aside.

"And a bag of ice."

"I heard you the first time." She took a bar towel, laid it out flat, and scooped ice into the center. She folded the edges of the towel over and twisted it like a wonton before handing it to me. "No bags, so you'll have to make do."

I took the ice and the drink and thanked her.

I pulled up my pant leg and saw my knee for the first time. The skin was already turning a dark shade of blue, and my kneecap looked swollen and out of place.

"Jesus," the woman said. "And I thought your face looked bad. You really did a number on it, didn't you?"

I told her I did, then reached for the drink, downed it, and set the empty glass on the bar.

"You owe me eight bucks for the drink." She motioned to my knee. "Ice is on the house."

"Start a tab?"

"A what?"

I looked around the bar. "Is Murphy here?"

The woman eyed me, didn't answer.

"I'm a friend of his," I said. "Is he in back?"

"I'd have to check."

"Do you mind?" I asked. "I'd do it myself, but—"

"Murphy?" The woman never took her eyes off me. "You back there?"

He answered, his voice muted through the wall. "What do you need?"

"Some sad-looking motherfucker out here wants to run a tab."

"Tell him to fuck off."

The woman smiled. "You heard the man."

I nodded, yelled back, "Brian?"

A moment later, I heard a chair scrape across the floor, then the door to the back room opened and Jimmy stood in the doorway.

He saw me and shook his head. "Yeah, it's him."

Brian said something I didn't quite hear, then Jimmy waved me back. "Come on, Matt."

I pointed to my leg. "That's going to be tough."

Jimmy stepped back and closed the door. I could hear them talking inside, then the door opened and Brian came out carrying an unlit cigar in his hand.

He saw me and stopped halfway. "What the hell happened to you?"

"Long story," I said. "Can we talk? Alone?"

Murphy turned to the woman behind the bar. "Rita, give us a minute, will ya?"

"I'm doing inventory."

"It can wait."

"Oh, for Christ's sake." Rita grabbed the clipboard, walked out from behind the bar, and disappeared into the back room, mumbling under her breath.

Murphy sat next to me at the bar, silent.

"I need your help," I said.

Murphy smiled. "I think you and I should get something straight." He motioned to the back room. "I heard about what you said to my brother. He didn't have to come talk to you. That was a courtesy."

"This isn't about that," I said. "I've got a real problem, and—"

"What else is new, Matt?" Murphy pointed at me with the cigar. "What was it last time? Losing your house, wasn't it? When is it not a real problem with you?"

"Jay came to me with a job," I said. "He had the whole thing planned out, but it didn't go the way we thought it would."

Murphy laughed. "Tell me you didn't get wrapped up in one of Jay's plans."

"Hold on, I—"

"Christ, Matt, you of all people should know better."

"Just listen."

"No, I'm not going to listen." Murphy sat up. "Things have been bad for you. I get it, and I'm happy to help out a friend, but only to a point. After the way you treated Jimmy, I'm starting to feel unappreciated. Do you even know the shit I have to do to cover for you?"

I started to argue, but Murphy held up one finger, stopping me.

"I'm not going to bail your ass out every time something goes wrong." He looked at my knee and shook his head. "You got into this with Jay, he can help you out."

"He can't," I said. "Not this time."

"Why not?" Murphy asked. "Where is he?"

"He's dead."

Murphy stopped talking.

"Roach, too, I think. I didn't see it, but—"

"Are you fucking with me?" Murphy stood up. "What do you mean he's dead?"

"He overdosed," I said. "Earlier today."

"Jesus Christ."

"But Roach—" I hesitated. "They killed her."

"Who killed her?"

I didn't say anything, not because I didn't want him to know, but because I didn't know where to begin.

"Matt?" Murphy slid the barstool closer and sat back down. His voice was slow, patient. "Who?"

"Roman Pinnell."

Something changed in Murphy's eyes, and his entire face grew tight and dark. It was like watching storm clouds pass in front of the sun. "You know who he is?"

Murphy nodded.

I waited for him to say something else. When he didn't, I said, "That's not all. There's more."

Murphy waited, silent.

"They took Anna." My throat closed on the words, and I swallowed hard. "They came into my house and took her out of her room, and I don't know where she is."

I could feel everything come to the surface, and I looked away, trying to keep the tears inside.

Murphy sat beside me for a moment longer, and neither of us said a word. Then he got up and walked around the bar. He grabbed the bottle of Jameson and a glass. He poured his drink then refilled mine.

"Roman Pinnell?" He stared at me. "Are you sure?"

I told him I was.

He nodded, then lifted his glass and drank.

I did the same.

Murphy set his empty glass on the bar and stared at it. He didn't say anything for a while. When he did speak, his voice was soft and cold.

"I think you should tell me about this job."

2 9

I talked for a while, going over how Jay first approached me with his plan, and how I eventually caved and agreed to help. I told him about Roach, the drugs, and how Jay had over-dosed on the floor of the warehouse.

"That was when Roach ran out."

"But you stayed."

"I thought I could salvage it," I said. "I thought I could pay you back, then grab Anna and leave the city."

Murphy frowned. "Finish the story."

I told him how I tried to meet with Pinnell to collect the money, and how he didn't show up. Then I told him about the phone call.

"He called you?"

"He had someone watching me," I said. "He knew exactly who I was, where I lived—all of it."

Murphy seemed to think about this for a moment, then he said, "He tracked the van."

I nodded. "How did you—"

"It's basic stuff, Matt."

There was an edge to that comment, and it cut deep. This was Murphy's way of telling me I'd been an idiot, and I was in over my head. He was right, and there was no way I could argue.

"I went home right away," I said. "That's when I saw what happened."

"And so you came here?"

"No." I looked up at him. "I called him again and tried to reason with him. I wanted to exchange his wife for my daughter. He told me to meet him in Pella Valley, so I went back to the warehouse—"

"Why Pella Valley?"

"I didn't ask," I said. "I only wanted her back. I would've gone anywhere he wanted."

"And he chose Pella Valley?"

I nodded. "The sheriff's department down there, they work for him."

Murphy frowned. "How do you know that?"

"It was a trap," I said. "Once he had his wife back, the deputies swarmed the place. Anna wasn't there."

"You were arrested?"

"They never arrested me," I said. "They threw me in a holding cell with his wife's driver." I hesitated. "They killed him in front of me."

"*What?*"

"I think Pinnell wanted to make an impression," I said. "He kept asking questions, wanting to know who I was working for, whose idea it had been. I told him it was only me and Jay, but he didn't believe me. He kept calling it a plot, an attack on his family. He was convinced someone else was involved."

"Was there anyone else?"

"Just Roach," I said. "It was her idea and his plan, start to finish."

"Blind luck."

I thought about it, nodded.

"What happened next?"

"They gave me some kind of drug." I pulled up my sleeve and showed him the bruise where the needle went in. "It could've been anything. It's all a haze."

"You don't know what you told him?"

"There was nothing I could've told him. I wasn't lying. I told him what I knew."

"And you don't remember anything?"

I shook my head. "Nothing."

Murphy turned and put the bottle of Jameson back on the shelf. "What exactly do you want me to do, Matt?"

"I want you to help me find my daughter," I said. "Help me get her back."

"Oh, is that it?" Murphy shook his head, laughed. "You have no idea who you're up against."

"I'm getting her back," I said. "I don't care if I have to go up against the devil himself."

"The devil himself." Murphy smiled. "That's not too far off."

"You know where he is?"

"Even if I did, I wouldn't—"

"Goddamn it." I slammed my fist on the bar and sat up fast. I felt the sudden movement in my knee, and I bit down hard against the pain. "I don't care if you help, but if you know where he is, or where he took my daughter, you have to tell me."

Murphy frowned.

I took a deep breath and tried to keep my voice calm. "I have to find him."

"Then what?" Murphy motioned to my leg. "You're in no shape to go after anyone, especially not Roman Pinnell."

"I don't have a choice."

Murphy watched me for a moment then said, "You know my old man worked for him a few times? Nothing big, but he saw enough to know what the guy was about."

I didn't say anything.

"He used to tell me stories when he was drunk," Murphy said. "Son of a bitch never said a word to me when he was sober, but once he had a few drinks in him, you couldn't shut him up."

"What did he tell you?"

"He told me Pinnell came up through the old South American cartels, and that he had his own way of doing things." Murphy paused. "I think it made him uncomfortable. He didn't say too much, but what he did say made an impression. I think he just had to tell someone."

"Was it that bad?"

Murphy looked at me. "Things I never dreamed of as a kid. It used to give me nightmares."

"And now he has my daughter."

Murphy watched me. "One thing doesn't make sense."

"What's that?"

"Why are you still alive?"

I didn't have an answer.

"I've been trying to think of someone who went up against Pinnell and survived, and there's no one." Murphy pointed at me. "Just you. Why is that?"

"I don't know."

"Did he say anything to you when they let you out?"

"They didn't exactly let me out."

Murphy frowned.

"One of the deputies," I said. "Just a kid. He let me go."

"He let you go?" Murphy stepped closer, leaned into the bar. "They beat you and drugged you then just let you walk out of a police holding cell?"

"The building was empty," I said. "It was only me and the kid. He saw what happened, and he didn't want any part of it. He told me if I didn't go, they were going to kill me."

Murphy stepped back and ran a hand through his hair. He looked past me toward the front door, then away. "So you walked out? Just like that?"

I nodded, not liking the way he made it sound.

Murphy seemed to think about this for a minute, then he turned and called for Jimmy. When Jimmy came out of the back room, Murphy said, "Go outside and have a look around. Let me know if you see anything."

"What am I looking for?"

"I don't know," he said. "Anything that shouldn't be there. You'll know if you see it."

Jimmy nodded and crossed the bar to the front door and walked out into the cold.

The ice on my knee was melting, soaking through the towel and dripping onto the floor. I took it off and set it on the bar. "What's going on?"

Murphy ignored me.

He walked over and reached under the register and took out a short-barreled shotgun.

"Murph?"

"Just wait until Jimmy gets back," he said. "I want to know what's out there."

"What are you thinking?"

"I don't know, but something doesn't feel right." He pulled a box of shells from under the register and started sliding them into the shotgun, one by one. "Pinnell doesn't let people just walk away."

"He wasn't there," I said. "He didn't know."

"Maybe not, but he knows now."

I frowned.

Murphy looked at me. "This isn't over."

3 0

"You're paranoid."

"Maybe." Murphy slid the last of the shells into the shotgun and tossed the empty box in the trash. "Maybe not."

"You think I was followed?"

"No idea," Murphy said. "All I know is that Roman Pinnell isn't careless, and he's not going to forget." He pointed at me with the shotgun. "They're coming for you."

"No," I said. "You're wrong."

Murphy ignored me and yelled toward the back room. "Rita?"

A minute later, the door opened and she leaned out. She had a clipboard in one hand, and her red hair was pulled back and tucked behind her ears, revealing a galaxy of tiny freckles that ran across her shoulders before disappearing under her shirt.

"Yeah?"

"It's probably nothing," Murphy said. "But I want you to be ready just in case."

Rita frowned. "Ready for what?"

Murphy didn't say anything, just held up the shotgun.

Rita's eyes went wide. "Oh, you've got to be kidding me." She came out into the bar and slapped the clipboard down on one of the tables. The sound was loud and it echoed through the empty room. "You promised me, Murphy. You promised."

"Special circumstances." Murphy walked around the bar toward the large front window and looked out into the cold. "Can't be helped."

Rita stood with her hands on her hips. She didn't say anything at first, then she turned to me. "This is you, isn't it?"

I looked at Murphy, but he was still staring out the front window and didn't notice. Even if he had, I didn't think he would've said anything.

I was on my own.

"Answer me, you limpy motherfucker." Rita stepped closer. "Things have been quiet around here for a long time now, and I want to keep it that way."

"I'm not—"

"You're not what?" She stared at me. "Huh?"

"Trying to cause trouble."

"No, you are trouble." Rita pointed. "The second you walked in, I saw it. Murphy, tell this friend of yours that we don't need—"

"Rita," Murphy said. "Shut the fuck up."

"What?"

"Why don't you head home?" He turned from the window and walked over to where she was standing and put his arm around her shoulder. "Take the rest of the night off. Go out the back. I'll meet you later."

Rita stared at him, not moving.

For the moment, I was forgotten.

"You promise?" Her voice was soft.

Murphy nodded, and she leaned up and kissed him, long.

When they broke, she glanced over at me and shook her head. Then she grabbed the clipboard off the table and walked through the door into the back room.

"Don't take forever, Murphy. I'll only wait so long."

A minute later, I heard a heavy door open somewhere in the back room. Then it slammed shut, and there was silence.

Murphy didn't look at me, and for a while we sat in silence. I watched him absently tap his thumb against the shotgun as he stared out at the front window.

"This isn't necessary," I said. "Even if you're right, they don't know I'm here."

Murphy pulled a chair from one of the tables and sat down, still facing the front. He didn't say a word.

"You think I'm wrong?" I asked.

"I'm not taking any chances."

"Why would they let me go?" I asked. "If they were finished with me, why not kill me?"

"Obviously they're not finished with you."

"I don't understand."

"You told me Pinnell thought someone else was involved. He even drugged you to find out who it was."

"There wasn't anyone else."

"And that's what you told him," Murphy said. "But this guy is meticulous. If he didn't get what he wanted from you in the cell, he'd try another way."

"You think they let me go so they could follow me?"

"That's right." Murphy smiled. "It's a smart idea."

"He thinks I'll lead him to whoever else was involved."

"And when you do, he steps in."

I paused. "I led him to Roach."

Murphy nodded. "Looks that way."

"Jesus."

"You didn't know," Murphy said. "And Roach wasn't exactly innocent. She knew what she was getting into."

"It's still my fault."

"Let it go. We've got bigger things to—"

A single shot sounded outside. The bullet came through the front window, spiderwebbing the glass and burying itself in the back wall. I jerked away from the barstool and crouched down, waiting for more gunshots, not caring about the pain in my knee.

Murphy stayed where he was, staring at the window. When no other shots came, he got up and carried the shotgun to the front of the bar. He looked out at the street for a long time.

"What do you see?"

Murphy reached up and touched the hole in the glass then turned and started back. "Come on, let's—"

Behind him, the front window exploded inward.

Murphy ducked at the sound and turned just as Jimmy came flying backward through the glass. He landed hard on the floor, and he didn't move.

I crouched in front of the bar and watched Murphy kneel next to Jimmy. I could see the blood covering Jimmy's chest, and the look on Murphy's face, and I knew.

Murphy made a short choking sound then stood up. He turned toward the shattered window, lifted the shotgun, and started firing into the darkness. He didn't stop until the gun clicked empty.

For a moment, nothing moved.

I pushed myself to standing. My knee throbbed under me, but it held under my weight.

"Brian," I said. "Let's go."

Murphy dropped the empty shotgun, then reached back and took a silver handgun from his belt and loaded a round into the chamber. He didn't move, just stood there, staring out at snow and shadow.

"Murphy?"

"Where are you, motherfucker!"

As if on cue, two silver canisters came in through the shattered window, both trailing lines of thick white smoke behind them. Immediately, my eyes began to water, and I struggled to breathe.

I grabbed Murphy's shirt. "Let's go."

Murphy didn't look at me. He was staring at the front of the bar, his eyes narrow, then wide. "Oh, shit."

I turned and saw three red laser-sight lines panning through the smoke.

3 1

"We've got to go. Now!"

Murphy lifted the handgun and fired several shots at the red lights, then we both ran through the door into the back room.

Once inside, Murphy shut the door and slid the bolt, locking it in place. I went for the emergency exit, but Murphy stopped me.

"No," he said. "They'll be watching the doors."

"Then what do we do?"

Murphy looked down at the gun in his hand and slid the clip out. He counted the rounds and popped it back in.

"Murphy?"

"You armed?"

I reached back and touched the gun in my belt and nodded. "We can't fight them, not here."

"The hell we can't."

"Don't be an idiot," I said. "We have to get out of here."

He didn't move, so I got up and took the gun from my belt and started for the emergency exit. If he was right, someone would be waiting on the other side of the door. I just hoped there weren't too many of them.

I reached down to push the lock bar on the door, but before I could, Murphy said, "Matt, over here."

He stepped back and knelt down beside the faded red-and-blue rug on the floor next to his desk. He lifted one corner and pulled it up. There was a trapdoor in the floor underneath. He unfastened two hook locks then pulled up on a small brass handle. The door creaked open, revealing a set of stairs leading down.

The air inside smelled wet and stale.

"What is this?"

"Storage cellar," Murphy said. "There's a light at the bottom and a ramp at the other end that leads up to a delivery door. It opens into a garage next door. I don't think they know about it."

"Then let's go."

"Jimmy's still out there."

"He's dead," I said. "Come on."

Murphy shook his head, stepped aside.

"If you stay here, they're going to kill you," I said. "We'll hit them back another time."

Murphy seemed to think about this. Then he shook his head. "You go. I'll make sure they don't follow."

I could hear voices on the other side of the door leading out into the bar, and for the first time I wondered why they weren't following us. "They should be in here by now," I said. "Something's not right. I don't like it."

Murphy stared at the door and nodded, silent.

I looked at the open cellar door and the stairs leading down and said, "We'll come back."

Murphy stayed focused on the door, ignoring me. Then he frowned and said, "Do you smell that?"

I could barely breathe through my nose. Smelling some-thing was out of the question, and I told him so.

Murphy stepped closer to the door leading out in the bar. He was staring at the ground. At first I didn't see what he was looking at, then I did.

A clear liquid came pouring in under the door and spread across the floor in all directions.

"Shit." Murphy backed up fast. "Go!"

I turned toward the cellar and started down the steps, hopping one at a time. Murphy followed. An instant later, I heard a loud rush of air, then a bright orange glow lit the steps and flashed hot against my skin as Murphy reached back and shut the cellar door.

I stood at the bottom of the stairs, letting my eyes adjust to the darkness. I could see the outline of a lightbulb hanging from the ceiling and I reached up and pulled the chain.

The light came on bright.

The cellar was long and stretched out under the length of the bar. There were several kegs stacked two high along one side, and a wall of empty cardboard beer boxes along the other.

Above us, the fire alarms screamed.

"Now what?" I asked.

Murphy pushed past me and waved for me to follow. We crossed through the cellar to the ramp at the other end. He pointed up to the delivery door and said, "My car is right outside that door. If we're lucky, they're not watching."

"And if they are?"

"Then we've got a problem."

I followed Murphy up the ramp. He hesitated only for a moment, then he pushed the door open and we stepped out.

There was no one there.

We were standing in an empty parking garage surrounded by cold light and cement.

"Come on," Murphy said. "Over here."

He ran along the wall and turned the corner. I did my best to keep up, but each step sent jagged bolts of pain through my bones, and I fell behind.

When I came around the corner, I heard the low rumble of an engine and felt it vibrate in my chest. The car, an orange 1969 GTO, sat alone, idling steady under a flickering row of fluorescent lights.

Murphy was sitting behind the wheel, and I limped around to the passenger side and climbed in. Before I closed the door, I heard the faraway whine of sirens.

I closed the door, and Murphy pulled out of the space and headed for the exit. When we got to the street, I looked over and saw the flames and smoke rolling up out of the bar before trailing off and fading into the black sky.

Three of Pinnell's men were standing out front watching it burn.

"Go," I said. "They'll see us."

"No, the fire's too bright."

I looked over at Murphy. The light from the flames glowed orange off his skin.

"We'll come back," I said. "Let's just go."

Murphy didn't say anything, and we sat there without saying a word.

The sirens were louder now. Still far away, but getting closer.

"Murphy?"

This time, he looked at me. It might've been the reflection of the fire, or maybe just the way the shadows fell across his face, but at that moment, I didn't recognize him at all.

"Are you okay?"

He didn't answer. Instead, he looked down at the dashboard, then reached out and shut off the headlights, dropping the car into darkness.

"What are you doing?"

Murphy hit the gas and pulled into the street. Instead of turning left toward the highway, he turned right toward the bar and the flames.

I braced against the dashboard. "Oh, shit."

The GTO's engine screamed, and I felt myself pushed back into the seat as the car picked up speed.

I saw Pinnell's men turn toward the sound, but they didn't move right away. The street was dark, and the fire was bright, and by the time they saw us, it was too late.

Two of the men were standing side by side, and they both turned at the last minute and tried to jump out of the way. Murphy swerved and caught them both head-on. They went down fast, and the car jumped as they passed under the tires.

The third man was farther down.

He saw everything.

When Murphy turned toward him, the man scrambled out of the street and up onto the sidewalk. Murphy pushed the gas to the floor, and the car tore forward. We hit the sidewalk hard, and there was a loud scrape of metal tearing against cement.

The man stepped back and lifted his gun. He fired one shot wide, then turned and ran, racing toward the corner of the building and safety.

He didn't make it.

Murphy caught him with the right fender, pinning him and smearing his lower half against the brick building. I watched the man's body bend backward and slam against the hood. He hung there for an instant, then Murphy turned and the man dropped away, landing hard on the cement behind us.

Murphy hit the brakes, and the GTO squealed to a stop. I looked over and saw him staring at the rearview mirror, frowning as the engine rumbled heavy and low. I started to tell him that we needed to leave before the cops showed up, but before I could, Murphy reached down and put the car in reverse.

"What are you doing?"

Murphy turned in his seat and looked out the back window. "Hold on."

I glanced around and saw the man he'd just hit lying on the sidewalk, slowly pulling himself along with his hands. His legs, bent and melted, dragged wet behind him.

I wanted to stop what was coming, but there was nothing I could do. It was too late.

Murphy hit the gas.

PART IV

3 2

We drove for a long time, crossing through the warehouse district to the lower market before merging in with the late-night traffic downtown. The dive bars and the dance clubs were closing and the streets were lined with people weaving their way through the crowds toward home, or whatever else the night had in store.

My hands were shaking, and I folded my arms across my chest to make them stop. I thought I should say something to Murphy, but I didn't know where to begin. I'd seen him angry before, but I'd never seen anything like what'd just happened, and I couldn't shake the idea that coming to him had been a mistake.

"Where are we going?" I asked.

"Nowhere," he said. "Not until I'm sure we're not being followed."

"Followed by who? There's no one left."

Murphy ignored me and kept driving. Eventually, we made it to the highway, and he got on heading north.

A few minutes passed before he said, "I want you to know that I don't blame you."

"Blame me?"

"For what happened to Jimmy." Murphy turned to me. "You came to me for help. You didn't know."

The shaking spread up my arms and into my chest. My teeth rattled in my mouth like loose bones.

I took a deep breath and did my best to steady myself. "Are you going to help me?"

"I'm going to do what needs to be done." Murphy cleared his throat. "If I can help you, I will, but he's going to answer for my brother."

"What are you going to do?"

Murphy shook his head. "I don't know yet. I need to make a few calls."

A few calls.

"To who?"

"That's my business," Murphy said. "You brought this to me, Matt. I didn't ask for it."

The tone of his voice was sharp, but I didn't care.

"Whatever you're planning, it has to wait until I have my daughter back."

I saw Murphy's eyes narrow. He turned to face me. The lines on his face were pulled tight, and his jaw worked back and forth.

I knew the look.

Usually, that look meant the start of something bad, but I didn't care. Murphy was big, and he could intimidate a lot of people, but I wasn't one of them, and he knew it.

"That's the priority," I said. "Everything else comes second."

Murphy's hands tightened on the steering wheel. He opened his mouth to say something, then stopped and stared out at the road. "And if you don't get her back?"

"I'll get her back."

"But if you don't?"

I didn't say anything. I couldn't bring myself to imagine not getting her back. The idea wouldn't even form in my head. There was no way I would let that happen.

"I'm only asking."

"I know," I said. "But I'm going to get her back."

"But—"

"If anything happens to her," I said, "anything at all, I'll kill him myself."

• • •

Murphy pulled up outside Conway Self Storage and typed the pass code into the keypad. The black metal gate whined and slid open along tracks buried in the ground. We pulled in and drove through a maze of storage units, stopping somewhere in the middle.

He parked and we got out.

Murphy took a phone from his pocket and said, "I'm going to make a call. It won't take long."

"You want me to wait out here?"

Murphy shook his head and flipped through his keys. He stopped at one, slid it off the ring, and tossed it to me.

"What's this?"

"Two seventeen." He pointed toward a block of storage units on my right. "It's about halfway down on the left. Go in and grab whatever you want. I'll meet you in a few minutes, and we'll talk."

"Grab what? I don't—"

But Murphy had already turned away. I watched as he dialed a number and pressed the phone to his ear before rounding the corner and disappearing in the shadows.

I looked down at the key in my hand and started walking. My knee was stiff and sore. I still couldn't put my full weight on it, but being off of it for a while had helped. I wasn't ready to run a marathon, but I thought I could make it to the storage unit without much trouble.

Two seventeen was a medium-sized unit, about as big as a one-car garage. There was a padlock at the bottom and I eased myself down and slid the key in.

The lock popped open.

I took it off and pulled up on the handle. The door opened easily. It was dark inside, and all I could see was a wall of cardboard boxes.

I felt along the side for a light switch. I found one, flipped it, and a line of fluorescent lights flickered to life above me.

I stepped back and looked at the boxes. They were stacked from floor to ceiling, sealed with packing tape and labeled in heavy black marker. I read a few. *Dishes*, *Photos*, *Clothes*, *Papers*, and *Books*. Another was labeled *Bar*, and one just said *Misc*.

I whispered, "What the hell is this?"

I stepped in and pushed on them. They were heavy and full. Along the far side, there was enough room to squeeze in behind the boxes, so I turned sideways and slid through.

There was another wall of boxes behind the first, all stacked and labeled just like the others. I followed the path around these, winding through the maze, leading to the rear of the unit.

Behind the second wall of boxes was a wooden table pressed up against the back wall and covered with a heavy blue tarp. I stood for a moment, staring, then reached out and lifted the corner of the tarp.

Underneath was an AK-47.

I pulled the tarp all the way off.

There were three more AK-47s, side by side, four Mossberg 500 tactical shotguns, and two rows of handguns, mostly .45s.

"Jesus."

At the top edge of the table, lined in a row, were three metal military-issue boxes stamped with the words *Frag, Delay, M67.*

I popped the lid on one and looked inside.

Nine hand grenades.

I closed the box and picked up one of the shotguns and turned it over, running my hand over the smooth metal barrel. I hadn't seen weapons like these since the Marines, and as much as I wanted to put those years behind me, there was something comforting about seeing all that firepower sitting right in front of me.

"What do you think?"

I'd been lost in what I was seeing, and the sound of Murphy's voice startled me. I turned around fast.

Murphy held up his hands. "Easy there." He pointed to the shotgun and smiled. "Nice, isn't it?"

I looked down at the gun and nodded. "Where did you—" I stopped. "Never mind, I don't want to know."

"No, you don't." Murphy walked over and stood next to me. He picked up one of the .45s, sighted it, and said, "Everything's set. We're meeting in an hour."

"With who?"

"Who do you think?"

I closed my eyes. "Oh, Christ."

"They had to know." Murphy set the gun back on the table with the others. "They had a big stake in the place, and they're going to want it cleaned up." He paused. "This is a good thing, Matt, don't worry."

"As long as they understand the situation," I said. "Nothing happens until I have her back."

Murphy took the shotgun I was holding and nodded. "I know the situation."

"I'm serious, I can't—"

"It's going to be fine, Matt. These guys are pros." He handed the gun back. "We'll both get what we want."

3 3

Murphy arranged for us to meet at an all-night diner just outside the city. It was late when we got there, and the restaurant was quiet. The only other people inside were two truck drivers, both sitting silent and alone at either end of the counter.

We picked a booth in the corner by the windows. There was a purple flower in a small glass vase on the table. I slid it to the side and stared out at the cars passing along the highway. Their lights were clear and bright and shone through the glass like tiny jewels.

A waitress in a brown-and-yellow uniform came up with menus and asked, "Something to drink?"

Murphy said, "Coffee."

I shook my head.

The waitress smiled a tired smile, told us she'd be back for our order, then walked away.

"When was the last time you ate?" Murphy asked.

I thought about it, but I couldn't remember.

"Get something," he said. "It's on me."

"I'm all right."

"You're going to need your strength."

I turned back to the window and stared at my reflection in the dark. Seeing it reminded me of Anna and the nights I spent with her in the ICU after the accident, watching her through the glass doors as she slept.

The thought turned black, and I looked away.

The waitress returned. She set a cup of coffee on the table in front of Murphy and took a ticket pad from her pocket. "What are we having?"

"Steak and eggs, rare, sunny." Murphy handed her his menu then motioned to me. "You decide?"

"Nothing for me."

Murphy frowned. "He'll have the same."

The waitress nodded and started back.

"And he'll take a coffee when you get a chance."

"You got it, hon."

Once she was gone, Murphy leaned back in the booth and said, "You look like you could use it."

I didn't feel like it, but I knew he was right.

"When they get here, let me talk." He lifted his cup, sipped. "They don't like strangers. It'll be better if you just listen and keep quiet."

"What did you tell them?"

"Only the name," Murphy said. "And what happened."

"Are you sure they'll help?"

"They'll help."

"How do you know?" I pointed to the window and the highway leading back to the city. "She's out there right now, and anything could be happening to her. I don't have time to waste with—"

"I asked them as a favor," Murphy said. "But you need to calm down before they get here. These guys are jumpy. If they see you acting like this, they might decide helping you isn't worth the risk. Then we'll both be fucked."

"But—"

"No." He tapped a finger on the table. "You need to understand something. After what happened tonight, I'm a target, too. We need their help to end this or we'll both end up dead. And your daughter—" He paused, shook his head.

I looked away.

"Trust me, Matt. This is our only option."

I thought about it, nodded.

"Good." Murphy lifted his coffee and sipped. "Don't worry. You'll feel better once you eat something."

• • •

But I couldn't eat.

After the waitress brought our food, all I could do was stare at it. The steak was bloody and blue, and the eggs rolled on the plate like two milky wet eyes.

But the coffee was perfect.

Murphy finished his eggs and was halfway through his steak when a rusted green Toyota pickup pulled up outside and two men got out.

Murphy had his head down and didn't notice.

"Is this them?"

He looked up, nodded, then slid over and said, "Come sit over here."

I pushed my plate across the table then got up and took the seat next to him.

The two men came inside. Both were wearing heavy down coats. From where I sat, I didn't notice anything unusual about either of them. If I'd seen them on the street, I probably wouldn't have given them a second look.

They saw us and started across the dining room.

"Remember," Murphy said. "Let me talk."

When they got to the table, they took off their coats and sat down. They didn't introduce themselves, and neither of them looked directly at me.

"Thanks for coming," Murphy said.

The man across from me pointed and said, "Who's this?"

"Matt Caine, an old friend of mine." He looked at me. "Matt, these are the Vogler brothers. Leo and Eddie."

I nodded to them.

"Why's he here?" Leo asked.

"He's the reason we're all here."

They both looked at me. "You're the one who went up against Pinnell?"

I nodded.

Leo motioned to my face. "Looks like you didn't think that one through."

It wasn't a question, so I didn't answer.

"It's gone past that now," Murphy said. "This is a bigger problem. What did you find out?"

"Nothing we didn't already know," Leo said. "We put a couple guys outside his house tonight. That looks like our best spot."

"Matt says the police down there work for him."

Leo nodded. "We can still get to him."

"What do you have in mind?"

I sat and listened to them talk, waiting for Murphy to say something about Anna, but he never did. Instead, they went over the layout of Pinnell's property, possible security systems, and how they could get inside.

Finally, I'd had enough. "What about Anna?"

Murphy frowned.

"Who's Anna?" Leo asked. He looked at Murphy. "What's he talking about?"

"My daughter," I said. "Pinnell and his men took her, and I need your help to get her back."

Leo turned to Murphy. "What the fuck is this? You didn't say anything about no kid."

Murphy held up his hand. "It's a side thing, not—"

"A side thing?"

Murphy looked at me, his eyes sharp. "Matt."

"Listen," Leo said. "I think I get it. I've got kids myself. But we're not a fucking rescue crew, you got me?" He shook his head. "The fact is, if Pinnell took her, there's not going to be anyone to rescue. We need to focus on finding ways to get at him."

"Murphy?"

He shrugged. "It's something we've got to think about, Matt. If we overreach, we all lose."

"So this is your plan?" I asked. "Arm up and storm his house like a fucking assault team?"

"We're not going to storm anything," Leo said. "We can get onto the property without anyone noticing. Then, we wait. Once he shows, we step in, hit him, and get out."

"You think it's going to be that easy?"

"Not easy," he said. "But it's been done before."

I didn't say anything.

"You don't like it?"

"I don't think it'll work," I said. "And I want to talk to him before we do anything."

"Talk to him?" Leo smiled. "What do you think we're going to do, run into him on the street? Maybe we can walk up to him and say, 'Hey, where's the little girl?'" He laughed. "That's not the way this works."

I listened to them laugh and tried to stay calm. I could feel the situation slipping away from me, and I couldn't see a way to hold on. If I didn't figure something out, I was going to lose the chance to find her.

I closed my eyes and tried to settle my thoughts. When I opened them again, I saw the purple flower in the vase at the end of the table. Something about it pulled me in, and I stared at it for a long time and didn't say anything.

Leo kept talking.

"And that's another thing." He pointed at me. "If any of Pinnell's people see you, they'll shoot you on sight." He shook his head. "I don't know what you did to him, but whatever it was, you—"

I stopped listening.

I stayed focused on the flower, and soon Leo's words blended together and faded into noise. I couldn't help it. My thoughts kept returning to that tiny glass vase and the thin purple flower inside. Something about it wouldn't let me go, and I couldn't look away.

Eventually it came to me.

"Yo, Matt?"

Murphy's voice cut through, and I looked up. "What?"

"Did we lose you?" He frowned but didn't wait for an answer. "Listen, we've got to think big picture. I'm not saying we won't do what we can to find your little girl, but unless you have a better idea, this is how it's going to be."

I turned to Leo. "You said something about walking up to him on the street and talking to him."

"Yeah, that is not going to happen."

"Why not?" I asked.

Leo frowned. "Are you kidding?"

"No, I'm not," I said. "I think you're wrong."

Leo smiled, thin and slick. "Is that right?"

I nodded. "I think walking up to him is exactly what we're going to do."

3 4

The gates surrounding the Bent Tree Gardens opened at eight o'clock. We were the first ones in, and we parked at the far end of the lot and waited. The sun was up, hanging low on the horizon, and the light reflected bright off the fresh snow outside the arboretum.

Murphy took his coffee cup from the center console, popped the lid off, and sipped. Then he pointed to the bag on the floor and said, "Hand me one of those?"

I picked up the bag and passed it over.

He took out a doughnut and leaned back in the seat. "I can't believe I'm going along with this."

"It's our best shot."

"You realize the longer we wait, the less chance we have of getting to him."

I told him I did.

Murphy took a bite of the doughnut then offered the bag to me. I waved it off.

A few minutes later, a rusted green pickup pulled in and parked farther down. The doors opened, and the Vogler brothers got out. Eddie glanced around the lot then nodded toward us and started for the entrance.

"Are we set?"

"It appears so." Murphy pushed the rest of the doughnut into his mouth, took a big drink of the coffee, then opened the glove compartment and pulled out a black .45. "I'll see you inside."

"Remember," I said. "Not until I talk to him."

Murphy looked down at his watch. "How long are we going to give him?"

"I don't know," I said. "Until he shows up."

"And if he doesn't show?"

"He'll show."

I could tell he wanted to say something else, but he didn't. Instead, he clapped me on the shoulder then opened the car door and stepped out, leaving me alone.

I watched him cross the lot, coffee in hand, then head up the walk to the front of the arboretum. Before he went in, he stopped and took another drink, then he dropped the cup in the trash can outside the door and went inside.

I looked down at my hands in my lap. They were shaking, and I squeezed them together until they stopped.

I thought about what would happen if I was wrong and he didn't show up. It was too much to think about, and I pushed the thought away.

Pinnell had told me in the cell that he came here every morning, that he couldn't start his day without walking through these gardens. If that was true, I didn't see why today would be any different.

Another car pulled in and parked.

Three women, all wearing long coats and pastel-colored pants, got out and walked slowly to the entrance. They leaned into each other as they walked, talking at once.

A while later, a maintenance cart passed by on the sidewalk. There were snow shovels in the back, and the man driving didn't look up as he circled the building and disappeared around the curve.

My chest had begun to ache.

What if he wasn't coming? What if he'd followed through on his threat and Anna was truly gone?

What if I'd failed her again?

I felt the darkness form in my stomach and start to spread through me, screaming at me to do something, but the only thing left to do was wait.

I checked my watch.

It was almost nine o'clock, and still no sign of Pinnell. Part of me expected to see Murphy walk out of the arboretum, followed by the Vogler brothers, and tell me they were calling off the entire thing, that we'd waited long enough, that he wasn't coming.

But they didn't.

Instead, at two minutes past nine, a black Town Car pulled into the parking lot and parked near the front of the building. A man I thought I recognized from the cell in Pella Valley got out of the front and walked around to the back passenger side and opened the door.

A hand appeared holding a polished black cane, and then I saw a flash of short, silver hair.

Roman Pinnell had arrived.

• • •

I watched Pinnell and his driver walk in, but I didn't move right away. Instead, I stayed in the car for another minute and tried to settle my mind, but nothing I did seemed to help. That scared me. This had to go perfect. I couldn't fuck it up again.

I took a deep breath, then opened the door and stepped out under a perfectly still sky. I looked around, saw no one, and started walking across the parking lot toward the entrance to the arboretum.

My knee had been numb for a while, but each time I took a step, I could feel something pop behind the bones.

Inside the arboretum, the air was rich and warm and wet. There were three separate walkways leading away from the entrance, each one lined with trees and flowers and color. The stone walls were high and spaced with full-length arched windows that looked out over snow-covered gardens.

Above it all, long glass panes ran along the ceiling toward the domed center of the building. And under that, an enormous tree, bent and scarred by age, stretched up out of the earth toward the light.

I searched for any sign of Murphy or the Vogler brothers, but the gardens were deserted. The only person I saw was a young girl in thick-rimmed glasses sitting behind the information desk with a book open in front of her.

She didn't look at me.

I started down the main walkway toward the tree in the middle of the arboretum. There were several smaller paths that led off the walkway and disappeared into the dense gardens.

Pinnell could've been at the end of any of them.

When I got to the center, I stopped and followed the line of the tree up toward the dome and the shattering of light coming in through the curved glass. I could hear the slow rolling sound of running water from somewhere deep in the gardens, and I looked for the source.

I saw Murphy standing on the other side of the tree in front of a long passage of tall acacia trees. He motioned over his shoulder then walked off.

I made my way around to where he'd been standing and started down the path under a feathered arch of branches. At the end, the trees opened onto a secluded cove filled with rows of dense flowering plants, and large windows surrounding a clear pond filled with a rainbow of koi.

In front of the pond, there was a long wooden bench.

Roman Pinnell was sitting on one side of the bench with his back to me. He had his cane in front of him, and his hands were folded over the top.

I stepped forward and cleared my throat.

Pinnell lifted his head, but he didn't turn. An instant later, his driver stepped out and grabbed my coat and started pushing me down the passage.

"Wait," I said. "I want to talk to him."

He didn't listen.

I tried to push back, but the man's grip was strong, and I didn't have the leverage. Then, about halfway down the path, he stopped.

I turned and saw Murphy standing behind me. He had the .45 in his hand and he was pointing it at the driver's head. There was a black suppressor attached to the barrel.

"Let him go."

The driver didn't move. Instead, he stared at Murphy then looked back at me. When he did finally let go, his eyes never left mine.

I heard movement at the far end of the passage, then the Vogler brothers stepped forward. Eddie put a finger to his lips and grabbed the man by his shoulders and led him out of the passage, away from the old man.

Once they were gone, Murphy put the gun in his belt and handed me a cell phone and said, "Just hit Send."

"Are we set?"

"Yeah." He nodded. "But don't take too long."

3 5

When I stepped out from the walkway, Pinnell was standing beside the bench, staring at me.

Neither of us moved.

Then I said, "I want to talk."

Pinnell didn't say anything, and at first I wasn't sure he would acknowledge me at all, but then he turned and eased himself down onto the bench.

I approached slowly, trying to keep as much weight off my bad knee as I could.

Pinnell watched me, frowned, then opened his hand and waved it over the open seat. "Sit down, Mr. Caine."

I sat and looked at the koi pond and watched the fish circle in flashes of red and gold and black. I thought about Murphy waiting for me, and I started to speak.

Pinnell cut me off. "I funded the construction of this building," he said. "All these gardens, actually. Did you know?"

I told him I didn't.

"The tree out there was here long before these gardens," he said. "Once there was nothing here but a field of grass and weeds and that one tree. I used to come with my son from time to time. I carved his name into the side of that tree. It's still there after all these years."

"My daughter," I said. "Where is she?"

Pinnell ignored me.

"Of course, when I donated the money for these gardens, I made sure they were built around that tree. There was resistance, but cutting it down was not an option, and in the end—"

"Fuck that tree."

Pinnell stopped talking and turned to face me.

"Where is she?" I asked. "I'm not alone this time, and if I don't get an answer from you, I'll—"

"You'll do what?" His eyes narrowed. "Blindfold me? Handcuff me to a pipe like an animal? Will you leave me to rot in some damp shed by the river? Will you beat me?" He hesitated. "Is that what you'll do?"

My throat felt tight, and when I found my voice, I said, "I didn't want her to get hurt. I went along to make sure she was safe."

"You went along out of greed and cowardice," he said. "Don't pretend to be something you're not. It's much too late in the game for that kind of illusion."

He was right, and there was nothing I could say.

"I gave up pretending a long time ago," Pinnell said. "I know my role in this life, and it's something I no longer try to escape." He looked up and nodded. "On one hand, I am the man who built this building, and others, in an attempt to bring happiness to people, but that is not all I am."

"I figured that out."

Pinnell kept looking up, seemingly lost in thought. When he came back, his voice was soft.

"I knew the second I saw you here that you weren't alone." He turned to me. "You're not an unintelligent man. At first, I thought perhaps you were, but I misjudged you."

"Where is she?"

"She's safe."

The words filled me with hope, but only for a second. I wanted to believe him, but I'd believed him before, and I couldn't do it again. This time, I needed more. "Tell me where she is."

Pinnell looked down and tapped the end of his cane on the ground. "I've done many things in life that I'm not proud of," he said. "But every action I took, every one, was for my family."

Somewhere, far off, a woman coughed.

The sound echoed.

"But one thing I've learned, Mr. Caine, is that you can never fully protect the ones you love. You can build walls around them, hire an army to watch over them, but eventually, something will get through." He pointed at me. "It could be a blind dog running on luck, like you, or it could be something else. Something bigger, something that sneaks in unnoticed and slowly drains away an entire life before it is ever lived."

"I don't see—"

"Or maybe something as simple as a car accident." He turned to face me. "Perhaps an overworked nineteen-year-old university student runs a red light one morning after her eyes drift shut for an instant while driving to class."

I felt the air rush out of me.

"There are a great many tragedies in this world, Mr. Caine. Yours is but one."

"How did you know about the accident?"

Pinnell looked away. "If I tell you where to find your daughter, what is stopping them from killing me?"

I was still thinking about the accident, and it took me a minute to pull myself together.

Once I did, I said, "Nothing."

"Then you're asking me to trust you?"

"I'm not asking for anything," I said. "I'm telling you the situation."

Pinnell sat up, exhaled sharp. "The way I see it, as long as I have something you want, I'm safe. Forgive me if I'm not willing to give up my one remaining chip on faith."

I leaned forward, resting my elbows on my knees, and nodded. "No, I didn't think you would."

"My suggestion would be for you and me to leave here together." He turned toward me. "I can take you to your daughter, and then we part ways."

"That's not going to happen."

"Then we are at an impasse." He tapped his cane on the ground and pushed himself up. "It's getting late, and I have a busy day. Right now I'm going to walk out to my car, with my driver, and we're going to leave. If you'd like to see your daughter alive again, I suggest you make sure we're able to do so with no interference."

I watched him as he spoke, and I did my best to keep the rage building inside me from boiling over. I told myself he was the only one who knew where Anna was, and if I was going to find her again, I needed him alive.

"Good-bye, Mr. Caine."

Pinnell turned to leave, but I stopped him.

"Hold on." I took the cell phone from my pocket and held it up. "You might want to sit back down."

"We have nothing else to discuss."

He started toward the passage, but he didn't get far.

Murphy stepped out, blocking the exit. He had his hands folded in front of him. He was holding the .45.

"There is one thing." I opened the phone and hit Send. There was a series of beeps as the preset number dialed. "We were able to intercept your wife before she left for the airport. Would you like to talk to her?"

Pinnell stared at me. "You're lying."

I put the phone to my ear. A man answered after the second ring, and I told him to put her on. He did, and I held out the phone. "I think she'd like to hear from you."

This time, something in his face changed, and for a second, I thought I saw his jaw tremble. Whether it was out of fear or anger, I didn't know.

Pinnell took the phone and held it to his ear. He didn't say anything, but I could hear a woman's voice speaking to him in Spanish.

He closed his eyes, and his shoulders seemed to sag under the weight of her voice. He turned away, whispered something I didn't quite hear, and flipped the phone shut.

He stood with his back to me and didn't speak.

"Like you, Mr. Pinnell, I also know some unpleasant men." I paused. "And right now, those men are at your house with your wife."

He turned to face me, and once again I saw his jaw tremble. Except this time, I knew it wasn't out of fear. This time, it was pure rage.

"Do you think you'll be able to run from me?" He lifted his cane and slammed it against the ground and yelled, "From me?"

His voice echoed off the high ceilings, and the sound seemed to snap him back. I watched his shoulders lift with his breath. Then he looked toward the windows and nodded.

"There is nowhere on this earth you will be able to hide if she is harmed."

"No one's going to hurt her." I stepped toward him. "As long as I get my daughter back."

He seemed to think about this for a moment, then he asked, "And as for me?"

"Not my decision."

Pinnell looked down and turned the phone over in his hand. "Do I have your word that she'll be safe?"

"You have my word."

A minute passed before he looked up and handed the phone back. "Then it looks like I don't have a choice."

3 6

I listened while he talked, not believing.

"You're lying."

Pinnell shook his head. "No, I'm not."

I watched him and I didn't look away. I thought if I stared at him long enough, he'd slip and I'd know for sure if he was telling the truth.

But he didn't slip.

Pinnell's face was stone.

I stepped back and opened the phone and hit Redial. It rang, but I knew no one would answer, not this time. They'd been given specific instructions: one call only. After that, no contact.

Still, I had to try.

I let it ring several times before I hung up.

"I assure you, she's there."

"If you're lying to me," I said. "If this is some—"

"I know what's at stake, Mr. Caine."

"I hope you do."

Pinnell sighed then moved back to the bench and sat down. He set his cane across his lap and said, "Since I am taking you on your word, I would like it if you took me on mine. We are both working toward the same goal."

"You expect me to believe she's been with you, at your home, this entire time?"

"It is the truth."

"You wouldn't take that risk."

"The risk was minimal," Pinnell said. "It was only to be one night."

"One night?"

"Any longer, and it would've become difficult to keep her in the country. We thought it would be better to—"

"In the country?"

Pinnell paused. "We thought it would be better to relocate her to a place with fewer eyes. Missing children in America attract a great deal of attention."

Nothing he was saying made sense, and I couldn't shake the feeling that it was all part of some game. Pinnell was too smart, too careful, and hiding Anna at his home was not only sloppy, it was dangerous.

"I can't believe you'd be that careless."

Pinnell looked down at the pond. "My wife was not the only one your friends stopped from reaching the airport this morning. Our plane was ready, and your daughter was scheduled to fly."

"What?"

"After what happened, what she witnessed, our choices were limited. She had to be removed, one way or another." He looked up at me. "My wife convinced me to choose the more humane option."

"You son of a bitch."

Pinnell set his cane between his feet and folded his hands over the top. "I hope, once you have your daughter back, you'll show the same compassion for my family that my wife has shown for yours."

I didn't know what to say, and for a long time, all I could do was stand there and stare at him.

After a while, he nodded toward the passage and said, "She's waiting for you, Mr. Caine."

• • •

Murphy was standing at the end of the path when I walked out.

I held out my hand, palm up. "I have to go."

Murphy looked at my hand then motioned past me toward the bench where Pinnell was sitting. "Did he tell you?"

"She's at his house."

"What?"

"I tried calling there, but—"

"They won't answer that line again."

I nodded. "I have his address."

"Do you believe him?"

"No choice."

"What if he's lying?" Murphy asked. "Are you prepared for that?"

I told him I was, but it wasn't true. Not only was I not prepared, I couldn't even bring myself to think about the possibility.

Murphy frowned. "The Vogler brothers aren't exactly patient, Matt. This is your only chance. If she's not there, I can't have you going off and—"

"She's there," I said. "He knows we'll only let his wife go if I get Anna back. He knows what's at stake."

"You told him we'd let her go?"

I hesitated. "I gave my word."

I could tell Murphy wanted to say something else, but instead he took his keys from his pocket and handed them to me. "Good luck."

I glanced down at the keys, then back up at Murphy. "I gave him my word, Brian."

Murphy stared at me and nodded, silent.

I started to tell him that they had to let her go, that she'd done nothing to deserve what'd happened to her. Then I remembered what Pinnell had told me when he had me in that cell, when I was begging him to let my daughter go.

Everyone suffers for those they love.

I didn't believe him then, but maybe he was right.

"I'll do what I can," Murphy said. "But all of this is out of your hands."

"I—"

Murphy shook his head. "Go."

I turned and walked away, my knee throbbing with each step. I wanted to run, not only to find Anna, but also to get away from Murphy and the Vogler brothers and what I knew was coming.

I circled around the old tree, under the dome, then started down the main path leading back toward the exit. I thought about Pinnell telling me how he'd carved his son's initials into the trunk, and I wondered if it was true.

I decided it didn't matter.

It would be impossible to find the spot without knowing exactly where to look. Still, I glanced over as I passed. I didn't see the initials, but I did see a small brass plaque set up in front of the tree.

I read it as I walked by:

Bent Tree Gardens
Sponsored by the Pediatric Cancer Foundation of
America, and dedicated in memory of Jeffrey Pinnell
1977 – 1982
Beloved son

3 7

The Vogler brothers' truck was still out front, but there was no sign of them or of Pinnell's driver.

I crossed the lot to Murphy's GTO, climbed in, and started the engine. When I pulled out of the parking lot, I turned toward the highway and headed south.

My arms felt weak, and my stomach rolled. I kept thinking about Anna and what I would do if she wasn't there. The more I thought about it, the more my thoughts turned dark, and the faster I drove.

I caught myself more than once and slowed down, but my mind kept spinning, and I knew I had to do something to stay calm.

I reached into my pocket and took out the cell phone.

I dialed Carrie's number.

She answered after the first ring.

"Oh, God, Matt." She talked fast. "That bar, it's all over the news. Someone burned it down, and they found bodies outside." Her voice cracked. "I didn't know if it was you or—"

"Carrie?"

"What the hell is going on, Matt? I didn't know where you were or how to call you." She took a breath. "I've picked up the phone so many times to call the police, but—"

"You can't do that."

"I know, I know." She exhaled into the phone. The air came out in stuttered clips. "Thank God you're safe."

"I'm safe."

"Anna?"

"I think I found out where she is," I said. "I'm on my way there now."

Carrie's voice broke, and I heard the tears come all at once.

She didn't say anything. She didn't need to.

"I don't have her yet," I said. "But I'll call you when I do, I promise."

Silence.

"Carrie?"

"I'm here." Her voice was quiet. "I just—"

"It's okay," I said. "Don't worry."

Again, silence.

"I'm sorry, for all of this." I hesitated. "I never meant to—"

"Just be safe, Matt." She stopped, and when she spoke next, her voice was steady and clear. "And bring her home."

• • •

Roman Pinnell's house was tucked up against a low hill covered in scrub oak. The lawn was long and framed on both sides by a tall privacy hedge. There was an oak tree out front, old and wide, and the snow-covered branches spread out over the yard in a canopy of white.

I drove by and parked a block over.

The house looked quiet, and the last thing I wanted to do was draw attention. I knew people in the neighborhood would notice a strange car parked at the curb, especially if that car was a battered orange GTO.

I got out and walked around to Pinnell's street and started toward the house. If my knee hurt, I didn't notice. All I could think about was seeing Anna, and even though there was no pain, each step felt heavier than the last.

When I got to the house, I started up the walk to the front door. There was a rustle in the hedge on the far side of the lawn, and when I looked over, dozens of blackbirds lifted into the air and scattered above me.

Tiny shadows against a chalk-white sky.

I stood on the porch and reached down to open the door, then stopped. It occurred to me that the men inside didn't know I was coming, and they didn't have any idea who I was. If I walked in without warning, things could turn bad fast.

I stepped back and rang the bell.

When no one answered, I leaned close to the window and looked inside, shielding the glare with my hands.

The house looked empty.

I could see a long couch and coffee table across from a stone fireplace with a gold peacock spark screen in front. There was a dark wood dining table at the far end of the room next to a glass china cabinet and a set of French doors that looked as if they opened out to the backyard.

Nothing moved.

I backed away from the window, opened the storm door, and knocked loud.

Again, no one answered.

I could feel the bad thoughts start to creep in, but I pushed them away and stepped off the porch and circled around to the side of the house.

There was a silver Lexus parked in the carport, and a door on the right side of the house. I walked up and knocked.

This time, when no one answered, I reached down and tried the knob.

It was locked.

The bad thoughts were stronger now and not as easy to push away. For the first time, I let myself think the unthinkable, and once I did, I couldn't stop.

I walked around the carport to a stone path leading up to a tall wooden fence. I didn't see a handle on the gate, so I reached over and felt for a latch. When I found it, I flipped it open and went through into the backyard.

The stone path continued along the house before turning toward a large brick patio with an outdoor fire pit and a tiered garden cut into the hill just beyond the yard.

I crossed the patio to the French doors and tried to pull them open, but they were locked. I could feel my body start to shake, and my thoughts start to slip away.

I had to stay focused.

I stepped back and looked around on the ground.

There were several large stones, about the size of grapefruits, lining the path leading up toward the tiered gardens. I picked one up and walked back to the French doors.

I found the glass pane next to the door handle then lifted the rock, ready to swing.

Before I could, I felt something cold and metal press against the back of my skull.

Then a voice, low and calm. "Put it down."

I dropped the rock.

3 8

The French doors opened, and the man behind me pushed me inside. I tripped over the doorjamb and went down hard. Several hands grabbed me, dragging me away from the doors and across a hard linoleum floor into a kitchen.

I tried to say something, but before I could, I felt a knee dig into my back, forcing all the air out of my lungs.

Then my hands were behind me, and I heard the long rip of duct tape. Once my hands were wrapped, the guy behind me stood up, and I sucked the air into my lungs, coughing, trying to speak.

"Wait, I—"

I tried to turn, but then the hands were on me again, dragging me up and across the floor. Someone opened a door, and I was pushed through. The floor under me gave way to nothing, and for a split second I felt myself fall, rolling down steps and landing hard on a cement floor.

I looked up toward the light at the top of the stairs and saw a dark figure, silhouetted in the doorway. He stared down at me as I tried to find my voice.

"My daughter, she's—"

The figure stood for a moment, then stepped back and slammed the door, leaving me in darkness.

• • •

Once I caught my breath, I rolled over and tried to work my way up off the floor. I managed to slide my legs under me and sit up.

The room was dark, and it took a while for my eyes to adjust. Even then, all I could see were dim shapes and shadows.

The tape around my wrists was tight, and my hands were turning numb. I sat forward and twisted them back and forth to get the blood flowing again.

It helped a little, but not much.

There was a thin slip of light coming from under the door at the top of the stairs, and I inched over. My left knee throbbed, and the pain was constant.

"Hey!" I shouted at the door, trying to keep my voice steady. "This is a mistake. I'm with Leo and Eddie."

I listened, but there was only silence.

"I'm the one who called," I said. "I'm working with Murphy. My daughter is here."

Still nothing.

I could feel all the anger and frustration build inside me, and it didn't take long for it to overflow. I screamed out and fought against the tape around my wrist.

"Open the fucking door!"

But they didn't, and I lost my balance and tipped sideways onto the cement. This time, my head landed on something soft. At first, I thought it was a pillow, or a pile of clothes. Then I felt something cold and wet against my cheek. An instant later, the smell hit.

Urine.

I jerked away, pushing myself across the floor.

There were two of them, their bodies lying side by side, legs folded together, barely visible in the shadows. I assumed they were Pinnell's men, but I didn't know for sure, and I didn't care.

I focused on my breathing and tried to keep calm.

I don't know how long I stayed there, but when the door at the top of the stairs finally opened, the light burned my eyes.

Two men came down the steps. They grabbed my shoulders and pulled me to my feet.

"This is a mistake," I said. "I'm—"

"Shut the fuck up."

One of the men got behind me, and I heard the click of a box cutter and felt the tape give way under it.

"What the fuck were you thinking coming here?"

"My daughter," I said. "She—"

But before I could get it out, they jerked me toward the stairs, and the pain in my knee sucked the breath out of me.

"What's wrong with you?"

I reached out and grabbed the railing beside the stairs and tried to catch my breath.

"My knee," I said. "I can't—"

The man with the box cutter shook his head and mumbled something under his breath then started back up the stairs.

The other one turned to me. He had a thin beard, scattered gray, and a curved white scar that ran along his upper lip toward the bottom of his nose. "Whatever's wrong with you, figure it out quick."

"My daughter is here," I said. "I have to—"

"Your daughter?" The man stared at me, and something in his eyes changed. "You're the one."

"Pinnell told me she was here."

"Did he now?" The man smiled and shook his head. "There's no kid here, pal."

• • •

"No."

I pushed past him and braced myself against the railing and climbed the steps into the kitchen. I walked through to the living room then down the hall, checking doors as I went.

The men followed behind me.

I heard my own voice, far away, like a whisper, repeating the same word over and over. "No. No. No."

I got to the end of the hall and felt a hand on my shoulder. When I turned, the guy who'd cut the tape from my hands was standing in front of me shaking his head.

"Not that one."

"She has to be here," I said. "He swore she was here. He knows we have his wife. He wouldn't risk her."

"What are you talking about?"

The man with the scar stepped in behind him and said, "He thinks his daughter is here."

"She *is* here," I said. "Where's his wife? She'll know, she'll tell me."

The man who cut the tape from my wrists looked past me toward the last door in the hall. It wasn't much, but it was enough.

I turned and grabbed the handle.

The man pulled back on my shoulder, but I was too close, and there was no way I was going to let him stop me.

I swung, catching him in the side of the head with my elbow. He staggered, and I grabbed his jacket and tried to sweep his legs out from under him, but the pain in my knee was too much, and I lost my balance.

The man twisted away and punched me hard in the chest, knocking the air out of my lungs. I felt myself fall, but before I could, he grabbed me, lifting me off my feet, and slammed me against the wall.

My head snapped back, and thousands of tiny pinpricks of light exploded behind my eyes. Then they faded, leaving only darkness.

"That's enough."

A voice, far away.

When I opened my eyes, the man holding me had his forearm pressed against my throat. He was looking over his shoulder at the other two standing in the hall.

I tried to pull his hand away, but it wouldn't move. I twisted against the wall, but he pushed harder, cutting off the air. Then I noticed the gun in his belt.

I reached down and pulled it out and pointed it at the center of his chest. I could feel my finger squeeze the trigger, but I didn't fire.

The man saw the gun, and his eyes went wide.

He stepped back, and for a minute, nobody moved.

My legs shook, and I pressed myself against the wall and tried to find my balance. My throat burned, and I reached up to rub the pain away with my free hand. Then I said, "I have to talk to her."

The three men stared at me. Then the one who'd had me against the wall stepped forward. He held out his hand and said, "Give me my gun, and you can talk—"

I pointed the gun at his head.

"Wait." He held up his hands. "We're all working together, right?"

"Out."

The men looked at each other, then the one with the scar stepped forward. "That's not going to happen."

I pointed the gun at him, but he didn't flinch.

"You can talk to her, but it doesn't change anything." He pointed to the door. "As soon as we get the word, we're leaving and we're taking her with us."

I stood there for a moment, then nodded.

The men turned and walked back down the hall.

3 9

I kept one hand pressed flat against the wall until my balance came back, then I reached down and opened the door.

The room was huge, lined with large floor-to-ceiling windows. There was a long dresser and mirror along one wall, and a king-size bed in the center, covered with several hand-stitched pillows.

Rose Pinnell was sitting on the end of the bed, watching me.

I crossed the room and stood in front of her.

She stared up at me, and for an instant I thought I saw her smile, more out of surprise than joy.

I knelt down in front of her and tried not to let the pain in my knee show on my face.

It didn't work.

"Is she here?" I asked.

Rose reached out and touched my chin, moving my face first to the left, then to the right. "My husband did this to you?"

I nodded.

"And your leg?"

"That was me."

She let her hand drop. "He takes things too far at times. It's a flaw he could never overcome." She paused. "Perhaps you're the same way."

"My daughter," I said. "Where is she?"

Rose looked past me toward the hall and didn't speak.

"Please," I said. "You have to tell me."

Before she could say anything, I heard a phone ring in the distance. Then there were footsteps.

I looked at Rose. "Please."

This time when she smiled, there was light behind her eyes. She leaned in close. "I hid her away." She took my hand and pressed something metal into my palm.

I looked down and saw a silver key.

"Don't let them know she's here." She motioned toward the door. "I don't want them to—"

The three men came into the room. They stopped in the doorway, waiting. I stood and moved to the side. Two of them took Rose, one on each arm, then the one with the scar said, "It's time. We've got to move."

Rose didn't say anything, and she didn't fight.

"Nothing happens to her," I said. "We have a deal."

They ignored me and walked her out of the room and down the hall toward the kitchen and the silver Lexus parked in the carport.

I followed.

Once they stepped outside, the man with the scar stopped and looked back at me. "I wouldn't stick around if I were you." He circled one finger in the air. "These neighbors, lots of eyes."

I stood in the carport and watched them climb into the Lexus and back down the driveway. I waited until they'd pulled out onto the street before I opened my hand and looked down at the key.

• • •

I went through the house again, checking every door.

None of them were locked, and all the rooms I searched were empty. When I got back to the main bedroom, I sat on the edge of the bed and turned the key over in my hand.

It was silver, plain, and had no markings on it at all, not even a scratch.

I thought about getting up and searching the rooms again. I told myself I must've missed something—a closet or a door—but I knew I hadn't. I'd gone through all the rooms, searched every corner, anyplace Anna could've fit.

She wasn't there.

I leaned forward and held my head in my hands. I tried to retrace my steps, going back through each room in my mind—four bedrooms, three bathrooms, two living rooms, the cellar—trying to see if there was something I'd overlooked.

Then I opened my eyes and looked up at the ceiling.

I'd noticed it earlier, but I didn't think anything of it at the time. I stood and walked out of the bedroom, never taking my eyes off the ceiling.

"Come on," I said. "Come on."

I came around the corner into the hall and saw the keyhole in the center of the ceiling. It'd been painted over and didn't stand out, but it was there.

I looked around for something to stand on. The hallway was empty, so I went to the kitchen and grabbed a chair from the table and set it under the keyhole and climbed up.

I slid the key in and turned it. There was a soft click, then a section of the ceiling dropped two inches, and I saw a leather strap tucked in along the edge.

I grabbed it and pulled.

The door in the ceiling came down at an angle toward the floor. I stepped off the chair and eased it the rest of the way. There was a folded ladder belted onto the top. I undid the latch and let it slide down and lock into place.

"Anna?"

Silence.

I started up the ladder, pulling myself along, one rung to the next. When I got to the top, I could see the midday light slanting in through the round window at the far end of the attic. But I didn't see Anna.

There were boxes and coatracks lined with clothes, and a child's bed leaning against the far wall. There were framed photographs stacked on shelves, picture books, a rocking chair, and a tricycle, red and rusted in the corner. All of it covered with a thin layer of dust.

"Anna?"

The ceiling was low, and I crouched down as I moved from one end of the attic to the other. I looked beside boxes and dug through piles of quilts and old clothes, moving faster, feeling the shallow in-and-out of my breath.

Then I saw something move under the coatrack.

A small foot in a small shoe.

I ran over and pushed the clothes to the side.

Anna was sitting on the floor, and when she saw me, she jumped back, pressing herself against the wall.

Her hands were tied in front of her with a long red scarf, and there was another wrapped around her head, covering her mouth.

I dropped down in front of her and reached for the scarf around her mouth. When I pulled it away, Anna looked up at me, her eyes wet and wide.

"Daddy?"

PART V

4 0

New development in local murder case
By Evelyn White (AP)

While investigating the shocking murder of a local philan-thropist, police have uncovered what may be proof of the victim's ties to organized crime, including several South American drug cartels.

Since the body of Roman Pinnell was discovered in the frozen lake outside the Bent Tree Gardens last month, investigators have been frantically searching for any clues as to why such a beloved local figure would be the victim of what appeared to be a senseless crime. But what they uncovered has turned grief into shock and rattled the tight-knit community of Pella Valley, where Pinnell spent the last 40 years.

Sources report that Pinnell, through multiple business dealings, can be linked to at least a dozen crimes, rang-ing from drug smuggling and corruption to extortion and murder.

Sources go on to say that in some cases there is enough evidence to not only implicate Pinnell, but also the Pella Valley Sheriff's Department in the crimes.

• • •

I finished the rest of the article then dropped the paper on the cabinet and looked out across the empty room. The boxes were packed and lined up along the wall, ready to be moved. The furniture was gone, and the floors had been mopped clean, leaving behind the chemically sweet smell of artificial pine.

The eviction notice had come earlier that month. At first, I considered fighting it, but I dropped that idea as quickly as it'd come. Too much had changed, and I didn't see a reason to stay, not anymore. At the time, it felt like the right decision, but now that the day had arrived, and I was left to face the empty rooms, I wondered if I'd made a mistake.

I thought about Beth and our first few nights in the house, how we'd slept on an air mattress in the living room while we had waited for our new bed to arrive.

I remembered the two of us lying together, staring up at the ceiling, and talking about all the things we were going to do. Beth had loved the house and saw how beautiful it could be. I thought of the way she rolled over and leaned against my chest and looked up at me in that way she had of looking at me, and said, "You know, that back room would make a great nursery."

The idea had been both terrifying and beautiful.

I don't remember what I said, but whatever it was, it'd made her smile and kiss me and say, "Don't worry, Matt. Someday."

Someday.

I looked down at the wedding ring on my finger and slipped it off. I turned it over in my hand then put it in my pocket and reached for the newspaper.

I found the article I'd been reading and separated it from the rest of the paper. There was a photo of Roman Pinnell at the top, and I unfolded it and laid it out flat over the plastic base of the pet carrier.

I whistled.

I heard the small sound of claws on the living room floor. Then a tiny face peeked around the corner and stared at me.

"There you are."

I reached down to pick him up.

The puppy turned and tried to scamper away, but his legs slipped under him, and he didn't get far. I grabbed him and set him on the paper inside the carrier. As I did, he growled at me, showed teeth.

Exactly how it should be.

• • •

I'd bought a used Jeep earlier that month, and it was parked out front by the curb. It had a few too many miles on it, but it was still in good enough shape to get me where I needed to go.

I opened the passenger-side door and set the carrier on the floor in front of the seat. The puppy was whining, and I leaned in and made a soft clicking sound with my tongue and said, "Don't worry, buddy. Not much longer."

I stepped back and closed the door and walked around to the driver's side. As I did, I glanced over at Carrie's house across the street.

She was standing in the doorway.

I stood there for a moment then raised a hand and waved.

She opened the screen door and stepped out onto the porch, her arms folded across her chest.

I crossed the street and walked up to the bottom of the stairs. Along the way I tried to think of something to say, but when I got there, all I managed was, "Hi."

Carrie tried to smile, but it didn't work. "Did you decide where you'll go?" she asked.

"I'll stay with Murphy for a couple weeks until I find a place," I said. "I've got an application in for an apartment downtown, but we'll see."

"But you're staying in town?"

I told her I was, then added, "For Anna."

Carrie nodded and looked away.

"I'm not going far," I said. "Maybe sometime, if you feel like it, you and I could—"

Carrie held up one hand, stopping me. When she looked up, her eyes shone wet.

I didn't say anything else.

"When you see her, tell her I said hello and that I love her. Will you do that for me?"

"Carrie, come on."

She reached up and ran her fingers under her eyes and said, "You should go."

I started up the first step, but Carrie moved back, shaking her head. "No, don't."

"I just—"

"No, Matt." She stared at me, and there was nothing left for me in her eyes. "I can't. Not anymore."

I stepped back, and for a while, we didn't speak.

Then I said, "I'm sorry."

"I know." Carrie turned and opened the door. She went in halfway then looked back. "Make sure to tell her? It means a lot to me."

"Okay," I said. "I'll tell her."

Once again, Carrie tried to smile.

This time she got closer.

"Good-bye, Matt."

41

I drove out of the city, through spring fields and horse pastures, then up into the hills. I followed the road through miles of trees and brush until it opened next to a perfectly still lake that unfurled like a sheet of silk, reflecting clear and blue under the morning sky.

When I got to the house, I turned in and followed the driveway up to the top of the hill and shut off the engine. I sat for a moment, not moving, trying to calm my nerves. Then I reached around and took the black polished cane from the backseat.

It'd been a gift from Murphy.

Since the surgery on my knee, I hadn't needed it as much, but I kept it with me just the same, and I had no intention of giving it up.

I got out of the Jeep and walked around to the passenger door and took the puppy out of the carrier. I ran my hand over his back then started walking up the driveway toward the house.

The front door opened and Dorothy walked out. She came down the steps, meeting me halfway.

"You can't just show up like this," she said. "You have to follow the rules."

"I'm not going to stay," I said. "I just came to drop him off. I can't take him with me."

Dorothy looked down at the puppy and frowned. "Another terrier?"

I held him up. "He doesn't like me very much."

"What's his name?"

"No idea," I said. "Not up to me."

"He looks like a Benjamin." Dorothy reached out and scratched him behind his ears and smiled. "Come on, she's around back."

We started walking up toward the side of the house, and neither of us said anything. I stared out at the trees, watching the way the sunlight shone green through the leaves and dripped warm and golden all around.

"How did it go with your friend?"

"The new bar opens next week."

"So the job is yours?"

"He wants me to manage the place until I can pay him back. I don't know what he's thinking. I've never managed a bar in my life."

"I'm sure you'll do a fine job," Dorothy said. "He obviously thinks you can. He must see something in you."

I'd managed to convince Murphy and the Vogler brothers to let me work off the debt. I had to sign my life away to do it, and I had no illusions about how long it would take.

"I'll be there for quite a while," I said.

"That's wonderful, Matt, I'm happy to hear it." She paused. "Once you're settled, maybe we can talk about overnight visits."

"Dorothy, I—"

"I'm not promising anything," she said. "But if you're stable, there's no reason why we can't discuss it."

I nodded, but I couldn't think about that, not yet.

Up ahead, I heard Anna's voice coming from behind the house. I stopped and looked down at the puppy. "Do you think she'll like him?"

"Are you worried she won't?"

"I don't know," I said. "He's not Dash."

"He doesn't have to be Dash."

"No, but those are big shoes to fill." I held the puppy up and looked at him. "Dash was perfect."

"He doesn't have to be perfect, Matt. He just has to be hers." Dorothy reached out and touched my arm. "She'll love him."

We walked around to the back of the house, and I saw Anna. She was holding a plastic bubble wand and running through the grass, spinning in the sunlight, leaving a scattered trail of bright soap bubbles behind her.

She didn't see me.

I looked over and saw Jerry sitting on the porch. He nodded, and I put a finger to my lips then bent and set the puppy on the ground.

He stared up at me and didn't move.

"Go say hello," I said.

The puppy looked from me to Anna. Then he saw the bubbles and started toward her. Slow at first, then faster, running up and racing around her, snapping at the air.

Anna stopped running and watched him spin around her. Then she dropped to her knees and patted her legs. The puppy jumped on her, licking her face as she laughed.

I stepped closer.

Anna looked up, and when she saw me, her eyes lit and her smile cut right through me. She lifted one hand, waved, then turned back to the puppy and laughed.

I felt my throat get tight, and when Dorothy came up and put her hand on my shoulder, I couldn't say a word.

Luckily, I didn't need to.

She understood.

"See," Dorothy said. "I told you."

ACKNOWLEDGMENTS

Thank you to Terry Goodman, David Downing, Jeff Belle, Danielle Marshall, Gracie Doyle, Reema Al-Zaben, and everyone on the Thomas & Mercer team for all their hard work and dedication. I'd especially like to thank Jacque Ben-Zekry for going above and beyond, and for making the publishing process with Thomas & Mercer so painless and fun. And thank you to Sarah Burningham at Little Bird publicity for being so damn good at what you do.

Thank you to my early readers, John Mantooth, Kurt Dinan, Ian Rogers, Christina Frans Lawler, Gill Rothwell, and Cindi Hermsen. It's much appreciated, guys.

Finally, I'd like to thank my wife, Amy, for her love and support. None of these books would exist without you.

ABOUT THE AUTHOR

 John Rector is the bestselling author of the novels *Lost Things*, *The Grove*, *The Cold Kiss*, and the 2012 International Thriller Award–nominated *Already Gone*. He resides in Omaha, Nebraska.